"I like your dress," Micah added in his still-businesslike voice.

"Thank you," Ella replied.

She should stop this going-nowhere conversation, change the subject herself, but instead she dropped her gaze to his lower face and idly noted that his beard was slightly thicker than it had been the day before and that his lower lip was fuller than his top lip. She wondered if he tasted like the coffee he drank earlier or the apple he'd crunched as a midmorning snack. Or a combination of both. She shouldn't be thinking of kissing him. He was her boss. She was advising him on a venue, trying to help him solve a pretty big problem...

Dammit.

"Problem?" Micah asked and Ella cursed herself to have let the mild oath leave her lips.

"No, I'm fine."

He pulled off his sunglasses and hooked them in the vee of his shirt. "Are you worried about being alone with me?"

"No, I'm not worried about you making a move on me."

His mouth lifted at the corners in a sexy smirk. "Then are *you* worried that *you* are going to make a move on *me*?"

Yes.

Scandals of the Le Roux Wedding

Will the bride say "I do"?

Thadie Le Roux's society wedding is set to be the biggest and most lavish South Africa has ever seen! Her twin billionaire brothers, Jago and Micah, will spare no expense, because family is everything *and* they have the Le Roux name to uphold.

And that certainly helps when things start to go wrong! A scathing social media campaign here, a canceled venue there... Will Thadie ever make it down the aisle? Not least considering all the Le Rouxs are about to discover that for a union to be binding, it must first be forged in red-hot attraction!

Read Jago and Dodi's story in
The Billionaire's One-Night Baby

Discover Micah and Ella's story in
The Powerful Boss She Craves

Both available now!

And look out for Thadie's story

Coming soon!

Joss Wood

THE POWERFUL BOSS SHE CRAVES

HARLEQUIN®
PRESENTS™

Recycling programs for this product may not exist in your area.

ISBN-13: 978-1-335-73869-1

The Powerful Boss She Craves

Harlequin Enterprises ULC
22 Adelaide St. West, 41st Floor
Toronto, Ontario M5H 4E3, Canada
www.Harlequin.com

Printed in U.S.A.

Joss Wood loves books and traveling—especially to the wild places of southern Africa and, well, anywhere. She's a wife, a mom to two teenagers and a slave to two cats. After a career in local economic development, she now writes full-time. Joss is a member of Romance Writers of America and Romance Writers of South Africa.

Books by Joss Wood

Harlequin Presents

The Rules of Their Red-Hot Reunion

Scandals of the Le Roux Wedding
The Billionaire's One-Night Baby

South Africa's Scandalous Billionaires

How to Undo the Proud Billionaire
How to Win the Wild Billionaire
How to Tempt the Off-Limits Billionaire

Harlequin Desire

Wrong Brother, Right Kiss
Lost and Found Heir
The Secret Heir Returns
Crossing Two Little Lines

Visit the Author Profile page
at Harlequin.com for more titles.

CHAPTER ONE

CAT MEME...RECIPE for lentil and lime salad...picture of a sunset...motivational quote...another cat meme...

Ella Yeung skimmed through her social media, bored to tears. She only had three weeks left at Le Roux Events—thank God—and the last month had been the longest of her life. She'd have stayed at home, as her boss wanted her to do, but pride had her clocking in to work every day. As long as she was an employee of Le Roux Events, she wanted Winters and his pet snake, Siba, the Human Resources officer, to see her face every day, to be reminded of how they'd failed her and, as she'd heard, a handful of other women over the years.

Being the cowards they were, if she walked into a room, they walked out of it.

Lately, Le Roux Events hadn't been a fun place to work but, in three weeks, when she was out of their hair, Ella had no doubt she and her complaints, would soon be forgotten.

Until Neville Pillay, their best client and beloved family entertainer, sexually harassed another woman working at the company. For how much longer would they protect him by sweeping his actions under the already filthy rug?

How—from Winters to Siba, to the Director of Human Resources at Le Roux International to the owners, the Le Roux brothers—could they live with themselves?

Over the past month, she'd tried to shed light on Pillay's despicable actions, but her complaints had gone nowhere and she hoped it didn't give him the confidence to be bolder, to push for more. Ella knew that he got off on feeling powerful and invincible, and prayed he wouldn't progress to serious sexual assault when the next event planner, secretary, make-up artist, backing singer or PA caught his attention.

It was only after her accusation had become public knowledge—within the company, at least—that she'd discovered he'd sexually harassed at least three other women at Le Roux Events. They'd all subsequently resigned, and Ella had no doubt he'd done the same elsewhere. But how was she supposed to stop him when upper management dismissed her claims and refused to take her seriously?

And, God, she was tired of trying. Tired of fighting. Tired of feeling alone and desperate to be believed. She'd taken her complaints to her boss, Winters, and then to Siba, the Human Resources officer. When it had been put to her that she hadn't actually been raped, that nothing *that* serious had happened—nothing serious? The man had put his hand up her skirt!—she'd emailed the Director of Human Resources of Le Roux

International, the sprawling international company that owned the company for which she worked, along with many others.

That fine individual had told her to pipe down, not to make trouble, and that if she kept quiet she'd be given a raise. When she'd refused to do that, she'd been offered a great package to resign. After she'd refused again, she'd been moved from her corner office to a small, cramped office at the far end of the building, which she shared with at least twenty dusty boxes, and had been given low priority events to organise—the events that were usually handed to interns for them to gain experience. Her Wi-Fi access was routinely cut off and her company car had been taken away.

It was obvious that they were trying to push out the trouble maker and, after six weeks, she'd finally cracked and submitted her resignation. Ella wasn't sure whether to feel relieved or angry that she'd buckled. But what she did feel was battered, powerless, less than.

Leaning back in her chair, Ella looked out of her window at the not-so-fabulous view of the car park, wondering yet again how her life had gone off the rails.

Not so long ago, she'd been a well-respected event planner in Durban with a reputation for getting the job done on time, within budget and with flair and pizzazz. She'd been working at a small start-up and, after successfully pulling off a couple of high-profile events, she'd been headhunted to join Le Roux Events, one of the best event-planning companies in the country.

She'd be based out of Johannesburg and her new salary and perks would be triple her salary.

It was, so they said, an opportunity not to be missed.

She'd accepted their offer and now, a year later, after having been promoted to Senior Event Planner, she was on her way out. Company management had closed ranks on her, and her colleagues avoided her. Oh, she knew they sympathised with what she was going through—and her female colleagues had sent her messages of support—but times were tough and nobody wanted to get on Winters' bad side. He was a 'you're either with me or you're my enemy' boss and nobody was prepared to risk losing their job by siding with her.

She got it—she did—they had mortgages to pay and families to feed. But it still hurt that she stood alone, fighting this battle not only for herself but also for the past, present and future female employees of the company. But such was the influence, spending power and star power of the company's biggest client.

Ella now knew—in a way she'd suspected before, but only now fully understood—that people only believed what they wanted to, that she couldn't rely on anyone to listen to her or to believe her, and that the only person she could rely on was herself.

Her dad had brushed off her opinion once and his inaction had been a factor in her mother's death. Now her boss refused to entertain her accusations against everyone's favourite client and the bigwigs of Le Roux International put profit and business ahead of their employees' welfare.

Her mum was dead and Predatory Pillay was still on the loose, free to make sexual, offensive comments to other women, to push them up against walls in empty conference rooms and shove his hand up dresses and between their legs...

Ella felt her throat close and her hands prickle and the papers she held fluttered to her desk. She would never have to have anything to do with him again. She was safe and, quite frankly, she'd been lucky. She had no doubt that, had that door not slammed, had they not heard the rumble of a cleaner pushing a cart, Pillay would've done worse...

She wondered if she'd missed any signs, something to suggest that he turned into a monster when no one else was around. But, as hard as she tried, she couldn't think of one instance that made her think he'd assault her; that he was anything other than the perfect gentleman he was reported to be.

Not only had she had been pinned against a wall and subjected to his roving hands but, because she refused to keep quiet, she'd been forced to quit her well-paying job and been branded a trouble maker. How could she be alone with a man again? Would she always be second-guessing herself, scared to take a chance, constantly wondering if this was another situation that would go south? How was she ever going to date a man again, take him home, go to bed with him?

Her faith and trust in people, never good, was now lost. Her trust in herself was shaky at best.

But, worse, what if Pillay did it again? What if the next time, someone didn't interrupt his assault and he raped a woman? Could she live with herself if that happened? But what more could she do? She'd tried to report him, tried to stop him. But she was just one person and Le Roux International was a multi-billion-dollar international company with tens of thousands of employees. She'd tried. That had to be enough.

But it wasn't.

Feeling helpless, and being disbelieved and dismissed made her remember what had happened fourteen years ago, when she'd screamed at her dad to listen to her. She'd begged him to take her mum to hospital, convinced something was very wrong with her suddenly sleepy, drunk-sounding mother. She'd begged, cried and yelled but, because her mum liked the odd lunchtime gin and tonic her father had opted to let her mum 'sleep it off'. Hours later, she had died dead from a massive brain bleed.

She couldn't help wondering, then and now, whether she'd used the wrong words or whether she hadn't expressed herself clearly. Had she been too emotional, not concise enough? Did it matter? Her mum's death had caused her to build strong, high walls. But the Le Roux management, by not believing her, had managed to scale what she'd thought were pretty good defences and flood her still sliced-up soul and unhealed open wounds with the emotional equivalent of hydrochloric acid.

Ella heard a door slam down the hallway and it jerked her out of her cycle of self-pity. Straightening her spine, she told herself to look to the future.

She didn't think anything remained for her in South

Africa. The event planning world was interconnected, and Winters had bad-mouthed her to anyone who would listen, from clients to suppliers and competitors. She'd been told that she now had a reputation for being difficult and a trouble maker. There was little chance she'd pick up another job at the same salary and level in the city. She could return to Durban—her father was still there—but what was the point when they didn't talk? Durban would also mean taking a massive cut in salary and smaller projects. It would be a step backwards.

No, her decision to emigrate to the UK was a good one. In a month, she'd be overseas, in a new city and, hopefully, in a new job. She'd have six thousand miles between herself and her dad, and she wouldn't feel obliged to see the man who didn't want to see her. London or Dublin would be a new start, some place where she could breathe and be herself again. And maybe, in a hundred years or so, she might find a man who'd support and believe her.

Then again, she might find a unicorn guarding a pot of gold first.

Through her open window, Ella heard the low growl of a powerful engine. Intrigued, she stood up and gasped when she saw a silver Bentley Bentayga turn into the car park. Before their relationship had fallen apart, Ella and her dad had shared a love of cars, with Ella spending many a Sunday attending car shows with him. The Bentayga was an exceptional SUV, stunningly expensive and, given its stratospheric price, there were only a few in the country.

She'd love to see one up close and personal and

she'd give her eye teeth to drive one. Ella watched as the driver expertly spun the huge car into a tight parking space. The door opened and a man exited, and Ella took a moment to admire his height: he had to be six-three or more, with wide shoulders, a broad back and a truly excellent butt. He wore a white shirt, his sleeves rolled up tanned forearms. His shirt was tucked into navy chino pants, held up by what looked like a soft leather belt the same colour as his leather brogues. His short, loose curls were expertly cut, a natural combination of light brown and the darkest blond. From the back, he was gorgeous. If his face matched his body, he could easily feature on the cover of *Men's Health*.

He turned to walk towards the entrance of their building—was he a potential client?—and Ella saw the thick stubble on his square jaw, strong eyebrows and sexy mouth. Yep, he had a masculine, fallen-angel face...

As if sensing her eyes on him, he abruptly stopped and tipped his head up, scanning the windows. Ella didn't pull back quickly enough and his eyes zeroed in on her, dark and dangerous. She couldn't tell the colour, but saw the intensity in his gaze, and she felt her skin prickle and heat.

She was so busted...

Ella blushed, lifted her hand in half a wave and saw his lips quirk upward in a 'I'm so hot what can I do?' smirk. He lifted two fingers to his temple in a cocky salute and Ella frowned, unimpressed with his attitude.

Sick of men who thought they were God's gift, she

opened her window and peered down. 'Get over yourself, I was just admiring your car,' she called to him.

Those strong eyebrows lifted and his smile broadened. Was that a dimple in his left cheek? *Yep, definitely overkill, God.*

'Really? I'm sure you don't even know what it is.'

Oh, God... His voice was warm and deep, a voice that spoke of an excellent education and old money. It was a bedroom voice...

Concentrate, Ella!

He'd just issued a challenge and it was one she could easily win. She intended to take Mr Cocky down a peg or two.

'It's a Bentley Bentayga, S-model and powered by a six-hundred-and-twenty-six horsepower, twelve-cylinder W-shaped engine. It has an eight-speed automatic transmission and is rated as the fastest SUV in the world. Although Lamborghini might dispute that claim, as the Urus SUV is also pretty exceptional.' As she expected, his mouth fell open and his expression changed to astonishment.

'Newsflash, Hotshot—girls can be interested in cars too,' she told him, before pulling her window closed.

God, she was so sick of being dismissed and underestimated! Sick of men who thought the world revolved around them.

Ella turned at a rap on her door and smiled when Janie, her closest friend at Le Roux Events, stepped into the room, her face alive with curiosity. 'Something big is going down,' she announced, her light brown eyes alive with curiosity.

Since she only had three weeks to go, Ella didn't much care. 'Has Paul in accounting received new hair plugs or did someone steal Eva's parking spot?' Ella asked.

'Neither,' Janie said, her eyes wide. 'Apparently the big boss is in the building!'

'Big boss?'

'Micah Le Roux, one of the owners!'

Ella frowned. The Le Roux brothers owned the events company but she'd never seen them on the premises. Her boss went to their offices, not the other way round. Janie walked over to the window and pointed to the car park below. Ella looked over her shoulder and saw a group of about five men standing by the Bentayga, discussing and admiring the car.

'That's his car, and Naomi just confirmed that he's here to see Ben. I wonder why?' Janie mused. 'Do you think it could have anything to do with your complaint?'

So the hot guy in the cool car was one of the owners of the company. Interesting. Ella recalled Janie's question and shook her head. She was too sensible to assume that. 'I doubt it. Even if he could be bothered, men like him, when discussing issues like mine, would demand a meeting in his office. He wouldn't drive across town weeks after the incident.'

'Then why do you think he's here?'

'I couldn't care less,' Ella answered. Why should she? She'd worked twelve-hour days for months and months, organised some incredible events and had come in on time and budget on every project. Le Roux

Events had made money off her hard work but when she'd asked for support, to be believed, they'd metaphorically punched her in the face.

It wasn't fair…and it most definitely wasn't right.

And, because he was on the premises and she had the opportunity, maybe it was time that someone told Micah Le Roux that straight to his face. Ella frowned, mentally asking herself if she really intended to confront the company owner…

For her peace of mind, she had to.

Would anything change? Probably not. Would she get an apology? That was wishful thinking. But Micah Le Roux would know exactly what she thought about his company, his managers and their abysmal attitude towards sexual harassment.

And maybe, just maybe, something she said would cause him to review their HR policies; to take the subject seriously.

She sent Janie what she hoped was a confident smile. 'Wish me luck.'

Janie's eyes widened. 'What are you going to do?'

'Ambush Micah Le Roux and give him several pieces of my mind.'

If he did nothing, changed nothing—as she expected him to—then she could leave this job and city, knowing she'd done everything she possibly could to prevent the same thing, or worse, happening to another woman.

Micah only allowed his smile to bloom, the first in days, when he knew he was out of sight of the gorgeous brown-eyed woman. A woman who knew a thing or two about cars, which upped her sexy factor by a good ten per cent.

He also liked her feisty attitude. He'd been firmly put back into his box and he couldn't remember the last time that had happened. As a Le Roux, one of the most powerful businessmen on the continent, that didn't happen often.

Or at all.

He'd felt her eyes on him the moment he'd left his car, had clocked the prickle on the back of his neck, the tingle in his palms. He'd scanned the building and quickly found her, standing at a window on the second floor.

He hadn't meant anything when he'd flashed her a smile and saluted her. He'd been acknowledging her presence but she'd taken it as him being flirtatious... Hell, maybe he had been. It was just what he did, a part of his charming persona. His twin, Jago, was meant to be the stand-offish and temperamental one, whereas Micah was seen to be more laid back, charming and personable.

That couldn't be further from the truth, though. He was the one who had to keep his temper leashed, his impulsivity in check, his quick tongue tempered. Charm and geniality were a cloak he could pull on and remove at will.

The woman at the window hadn't appreciated his casual, flirtatious attitude. Her eyebrows had pulled together, her wide mouth had thinned and she'd gripped the edge of the window sill a little tighter. He'd just stood there like an idiot, head tipped back, unable to walk away, entranced by her loveliness.

She was a startling combination of cultures—Chinese, white and maybe Indian. Her straight hair was the rich, deep, dark brown of imbuia wood. Her cheekbones were high, her mouth sensuous and her chin stubborn. Her body, the little of it he'd been able to see, was thin but curvy. She looked young—twenty-four, twenty-five—but her confidence and wit suggested she was older, probably in her late twenties or early thirties.

As he walked to the entrance, he wondered who she was. That she was one of his employees was indisputable—she was in his building, on a floor occupied by Le Roux Events staff. He didn't expect her to recognise him; few at this level did. Was she a clerk, an event planner, an accountant or did she work in admin? Did she like working at Le Roux Events? How long had she worked for them?

The urge to stop, to log into the Le Roux International server—the one that only he, Jago and a couple of their most senior and trusted employees had access to—and pull up her file was almost overwhelming. Since this small subsidiary only employed thirty or forty people, he'd find her quickly. In five minutes, he could know her age, her history, her credit score, her salary and see her work reviews.

Micah shook his head and ran his hand up and down his jaw. He'd never—not once since he'd started working for his father after graduating university—used his power and access to spy on an employee. Doing that would be a serious breach of trust. It was his and Jago's view that they only pulled an employee's record when they had damn good reason to.

And that reason had never occurred because they'd never interfered in the day-to-day running of the companies they owned. He and Jago had too many enterprises to do anything but look at company performance and balance sheets. He was only here because he had a very specific problem: he needed to find a new wedding venue for his sister's prestigious wedding in two months' time.

He didn't have time for an out-of-the-blue attraction, neither did he have the inclination. He had a company to run, deals to do, money to make. His responsibilities at Le Roux International required him to work sixteen-hour days as it was. Micah had no idea how he was going to fit in the search for a wedding venue on top of his insane workload. But he was, once again, taking responsibility for a problem that wasn't his...

But that was what he did, who he was. Whenever anything went wrong with his family, because of what he'd done twenty years ago, he assumed the responsibility of fixing the problem. Because he couldn't fix what had happened to Brianna...

Micah felt his breath catch in his throat and, needing a minute, he changed course and walked away from the entrance and down the side of the building, slipping round the corner and into a small alley between his and the next building. He leaned his back against the red brick wall, lifted his foot and placed it on the wall, tipping his face to the sun.

This month would be Brianna's twentieth year of

being in a persistent vegetative state, two decades of being non-responsive. She'd spent nearly seven thousand, five hundred days in that hospital bed on a feeding tube.

And it was his fault. He'd put her there.

Why the hell had he phoned her when he'd stormed out of Hadleigh House? Why had he dumped his hurt and anger on her? He knew the answer to that question: because she'd been the one person, besides Jago, who understood the screwed-up dynamics of the Le Roux family, and Jago hadn't been around. Their parents had been long-time friends. She'd grown up with Jago and him and had been part of the family. She'd seen Theo's temper, his need for control, and had often told Micah that his frequent fights with his father would end in tragedy.

She'd been right but she'd been the one who'd paid the price for his lack of control and blinding anger. Because she'd loved him, because she'd needed to rescue him, Brianna had followed him, and on a busy Johannesburg road had met her future. Or non-future.

The events of that night had changed everything. By far the worst consequence was Brianna's catastrophic head injury. But there'd been other consequences too: for the Pearson and Le Roux families, for his siblings and, obviously, for himself.

Naturally, he'd personally taken more than a few major hits. In the aftermath of the incident, he'd drunk far too much, flirted with drugs and had looked for any respite from the swamping guilt and unrelenting pain. Jago had got him some professional help—his father and stepmother hadn't bothered—and he'd cleaned up his act. He'd learned to control his temper and reckless streak, and had vowed that he'd do anything and everything to make life for his siblings flow smoothly—he'd be polite to his stepmother but she could take care of herself—vowing he'd never disappoint Jago or Thadie again. He'd also promised himself he'd never hurt another woman, in any way, ever again. As a result, he only ever engaged in shallow affairs, one-night stands.

Brianna had wanted the big family, the husband and the picket fence. At one point he'd wanted the dream too, but he didn't deserve to have what she couldn't, what he'd taken from her.

Guilt was his constant companion, his ever-faithful friend.

Micah gripped the bridge of his nose and squeezed. Standing here, thinking about the past—how he'd messed up so many lives—wasn't going to get his immediate problem solved.

His sister was getting married in two months and, a couple of days ago, some swamp rat had called the hotel hosting the wedding, somehow convinced everyone working there that he was representing Thadie's wedding planner and had cancelled the wedding reception. The organisation, believing the fake calls and emails, had immediately rebooked the space and now Thadie, Clyde and their thousand guests had nowhere to celebrate their union.

Thadie and her very expensive and famous wedding planner, Anna de Palmer-Whyte, had spent the past two days frantically calling round to find another venue but had yet to find anything suitable in and around the city. Seeing their rising panic, Micah had offered his assistance and to co-opt one of the event planners they employed to work with him to find a venue outside of the city. Yeah, he had deals pending and an overflowing inbox, but Thadie could ask him to pluck the moon from the sky and he'd find a way to do it. Thadie, her twin toddler boys and his own twin, Jago, were the most important people in his life, and he'd do anything for them. And apparently 'anything' included finding a five-star wedding venue.

Micah headed back to the entrance, his hands in the pockets of his trousers. Over the years he'd paid little attention to this business, one of many that was part of the empire he and Jago controlled. The place turned over a decent profit and it was handy to have a group of professionals on call to organise company events, which they did with efficiency and aplomb. He could've summoned the manager to his penthouse office in Sandton, but a personal visit would impress the urgency of the situation.

Hopefully, someone within the building would be able to find him that elusive, and exclusive, venue. Pulling open the front door, he glanced up to the second floor and felt a moment's regret at not seeing the gorgeous brunette again.

But he couldn't afford the time to be distracted.

CHAPTER TWO

BEN WINTERS DIDN'T have any event planners he could spare.

Micah sat across from his manager in his messy office—the guy needed to do some filing—and listened to him explain that his planners were all juggling two, three, sometimes even five projects in various stages. He couldn't spare anyone to research possible venues outside of the city and then travel to see whether they were suitable.

'The best I can do is to ask my planners whether they have any ideas, any contacts. Of course, it would help if I knew what type of function you are wanting to host...' Ben suggested.

He was fishing for information—obviously curious as to what could be so important and imminent to demand his involvement—but Micah rarely explained his actions. And it was a family rule that they never discussed personal matters with anyone who didn't share their DNA.

The sole exception to that rule was Jabu, their long-term butler, confidant, father figure and friend.

'Capacity to hold a thousand guests, sophisticated, upmarket. Ample accommodation in the area. Money is not an object,' Micah stated. He saw Ben scrunch up his face and shrug his shoulders, and realised that he'd wasted his morning visiting Le Roux Events. If Winters reflected the people he employed, then he'd receive no help from them. He needed someone to think creatively, to be innovative, and he didn't think he'd find that someone here.

Micah stood up. 'Thanks for your time,' he said, holding out his hand.

'I'll walk you out,' Ben said and mouthed a curse when his phone rang. He picked it up and looked at the screen and it was obvious to Micah that he wanted to take the call. He told Ben he'd see himself out.

Leaving his office, Micah ignored the flirty smile the receptionist sent him and pushed his hand through his hair. He genuinely didn't know what to do next, an unusual situation for him.

He'd head back to his office and maybe he and Jago could brainstorm some ideas. Two heads were always better than one. Pulling open the door, he stepped outside and felt the slap of the midday, somnolent summer heat. He pulled his phone from his pocket and checked his messages as he headed back to his car, desperate to climb inside and blast the air-conditioner. The vehicle had cost him a quarter of a million pounds—being an international company they only thought in pounds, not rands—but, right now, all he wanted from it was its ability to blow frigid air at his overheated body.

Micah used the key fob to open his driver door and

looked up from his phone to see the brunette from earlier leaning against his door. She wore a sleeveless pale-pink top tucked into a slimline black skirt that hit just above her knees, and killer heels. Some time in the last fifteen minutes she'd rearranged her long hair into a twist pinned to the back of her head with a clip.

Their eyes collided. Micah saw the rolling emotion in hers and sighed. She was great-looking—slim and lovely—but he didn't have the time to dally, or for a dalliance, right now.

And he was surprised that she was down here, waiting for him. He thought he'd annoyed her, but it wasn't the first time his surname had changed a woman's mind about his level of attractiveness. Sad but true.

'Can I help you?' he asked, keeping his tone cool.

'I doubt it,' she replied, her tone snippy. He looked again and saw that the emotion in her eyes wasn't desire but annoyance. Maybe even anger.

Right, he'd read her wrong. Which begged the question: what had he done to upset her?

'I'm Ella Yeung,' she stated, looking at him as if he should know her name.

He shrugged. 'Have we met before?'

'No, but I thought you would've read about me somewhere along the line.'

He had no idea what she was talking about. 'Look, I don't have time to play guessing games with you, Ms Yeung. If you have something to say, get on with it, because I have things to do and somewhere to be.'

Confusion and frustration ran across her face and Micah watched as she seemed to collapse in on herself.

She lifted her clenched fist to her mouth and the last remaining colour in her face faded. 'You don't know what happened to me, do you?'

Whatever it was, it was serious. He didn't know why or how but Micah knew he needed to hear it. He nodded to the entrance. 'Let's go inside where it's cool. I'll commandeer an office and you can tell me what's on your mind.'

Ella shook her head. 'No.' She crossed her arms and nodded at his driver's door. 'We can talk in your car.'

Micah walked her round to the passenger side, opened the door and waited for her to settle in the passenger seat. When he was behind the wheel, he turned the ignition and blasted the air-conditioner. The smell of new leather filled the car and he watched as Ella took in the interior, with its real wood trim and metal accents. She suited the car, he thought—classy and elegant. And, up close, she was sexier than he'd initially realised.

Micah took in her creamy complexion touched with a hint of magnolia, the exact colour of the flowers his mum so adored. He'd been right about her heritage, Chinese and Caucasian mostly, and stunning. Her cheekbones were high, her eyes an intense brown and shot with hints of gold and green. Her nose was long and straight. Her full mouth was covered in a pale pink lipstick, and even that hint of make-up was unnecessary.

Micah, used to attractive woman and not normally caught off-guard, swallowed and tried to ignore the way she ignited his desire. What the hell? Yeah, she had good hair—thick and a deep, dark brown—and a great body, but he'd dated supermodels, sports stars, actresses and aristocrats and nobody had ever, *ever*, caused his world to tilt, to knock him off-balance like this.

Calm down, Le Roux.

Ella leaned forward, adjusted the vents and ran her hand over the sleek dashboard in front of her. He expected her to compliment the car but the next words out of her mouth rocked his world.

'I've recently resigned from my position as an event planner for Le Roux Events. I did that because our biggest client, Neville Pillay, sexually accosted me.'

Pillay? He'd met him a few times and had liked the guy. He was said to be the most popular entertainer in the country and was respected as a philanthropist and actor. He looked at Ella and saw that her fists were clenched. Her expression was blank but the muscles in her neck were tight with tension. He'd lived with a consummate liar his entire life and could spot BS from a mile away. Micah knew Ella was telling the truth.

He chose his words carefully. 'I'm so sorry that happened to you, Ella. Did you report it to the police? To Ben Winters, Human Resources?'

Her laugh was high and false. 'Yes, I reported it. The police said that because there were no witnesses, and because it wasn't what they termed a serious assault, it was a "he said, she said" situation. Ben and Siba, our HR guy, suggested I gave him the wrong signals and asked me to forget it.'

They said fury was coloured red but to Micah, it was a deep black, and endless. He closed his eyes and asked another question. 'Start at the beginning and tell me everything, Ella. Every little thing.'

By the time she was done, Micah had learned that the company had been covering up Pillay's misdeeds for years, and that every single person to whom Ella had taken her problem had disappointed her.

He'd always been proud of the work he and his brother did and was proud of the company they'd built. Right up until this moment. He felt sick, ashamed and soul-deep, skin-exploding angry.

'I don't expect you to believe me—you have absolutely no reason to—but neither my brother nor I knew anything about this. It was never brought to our attention,' Micah told her, conscious of how weak his explanation sounded.

'I just wanted you to know, in the faint hope that you'll do something so that it doesn't happen again,' Ella told him, her hand looking for the door handle. 'I've resigned, so I'm out of here, but he might do something else, something worse, to someone down the line.'

'That won't happen,' Micah told her. 'I will fix this, I promise.'

She looked at him, her eyes deep and fathomless. 'I'd like to believe you, Mr Le Roux, but I've heard too many empty words and insincere promises from your company, and throughout my life, to believe anyone about anything.'

She slipped out of his car and, without looking at him, slammed the door closed. Micah watched as she walked back to his building, her spine straight and her chin up.

How the hell was he going to fix this?

He didn't know but he would. He'd do it for that proud young woman and, as she'd pointed out, for his future employees.

Micah instructed his on-board computer to call Jago and, when his twin's face appeared on the screen in front of him, he spoke. 'Do you know about a sexual harassment claim made by Ella Yeung, employed by us as an event planner?'

Jago frowned and shook his head. 'No. Should I?'

'Our Head of Human Resources does.'

Jago shrugged. 'Were our protocols followed and, more importantly, did our employee get counselling? Is she okay?'

Micah rubbed his temples with his fingertips. 'No. Nobody believed her, Jago. Because of the fame of her accuser, not one person in our organisation took her seriously.'

'Who harassed her?'

Micah told him and Jago's eyebrows flew up in shock. 'Well, he wasn't on my list of most likely of-fenders.'

'Mine neither but I believe her, Jay.' Damn, he hoped Jago stood with him on this, but if he didn't he'd go it alone. Their people had disappointed Ella but he wouldn't.

'Good enough for me,' Jago replied.

'I plan to take Pillay down, but that will take fi-nesse,' Micah told his twin, his tone resolute. 'But I intend to find out what went wrong in our organisation first. They branded Ella as a trouble maker and pretty much forced her to resign.'

'Right.' Jago's expression darkened and his navy eyes turned black with anger. 'What the hell, Micah? We have a policy, a protocol, and our employees' well-being always come first!'

'Not this time. Maybe you should alert the board, Jago, because heads are about to roll.'

Jago sent him a tight smile. 'Last time I checked, we own this company and we set the policy. Screw the board. I'll start sharpening the swords.'

Back in her office, Ella dropped into her chair, placed her elbows on her desk and pushed her fingers into her hair.

What on earth had happened out there? Instead of reading Micah Le Roux the riot act, instead of tearing off ten strips of skin, she'd caved and in fits and starts, told him the whole story.

Where had her fire gone? While she'd been waiting for him to appear, she'd built up a huge head of steam, but as soon as she looked into his Persian blue eyes her anger had faded and embarrassment strolled in.

Oh, she wasn't embarrassed about what had happened with Pillay; none of that was her fault and she refused to take any blame for any part of his appalling actions. But she felt embarrassed that her first conversation with Micah Le Roux had revolved around her being sexually accosted. She hadn't wanted him to see the tears in her eyes, to hear her halting voice.

She would've far preferred the big boss to be eighty years old and portly, not young, fit and gorgeous. She would've liked their first conversation to have happened at a bar, over a glass of chilled champagne, or at a restaurant over perfectly grilled fish. Or at a club with a sexy beat pulsing in the background.

All of which was insane. Even if Pillay was a choir boy, there would've been no chance of her meeting Micah Le Roux! She was just another working woman, one of the millions in the city; he was South African royalty. Their paths were never destined to cross again so why was she thinking about clashing gazes across champagne flutes, dancing with him in a nightclub or sharing getting-to-know-you dinners?

Why was she fantasising over his lovely blue eyes, his masculine face and stunning body? Maybe because she'd had so little to fantasise over lately…

But she should focus on his reaction which, to be honest, had been surprising. She'd expected him to find excuses, to play down what happened to her, but he'd seemed genuinely angry—completely horrified, in fact. Ella did not doubt that her claims had been a surprise to him: she'd seen his shocked, then furious, expression.

But what she did doubt was his promise to fix the situation. She didn't believe him, she couldn't. She'd been let down too often by too many people to put her faith in a stranger, even if he was rich and sexy, made her stomach pitch and roll and her heart flutter.

Besides, what would he fix? Sure, he could fire everyone who'd ignored her claim—not a likely scenario, admittedly—but there was little he could do about Neville Pillay, as going after him would be a PR nightmare. He was a very popular entertainer, known to be a loving family man, and nobody would believe that a snake lurked beneath his designer clothes. Micah publicly accusing him of sexual harassment would damage the Le Roux brand and that wasn't something a successful billionaire businessman would do. Not on the word of one mid-level employee.

It was done and she should just try to put the last few months behind her. There wasn't anything more she could do and it was obvious that she'd never see Micah Le Roux again.

It was time to focus on the future, to make a new life somewhere else. She just needed to hang in here a little longer. If she did, she'd be paid her bi-annual performance bonus. She'd endured so much already. She could handle another fifteen working days spent in this cramped and stuffy room.

Two days later, Micah was back at Le Roux Events. After checking that Winters' office was empty, he walked up the stairs to the second floor, ended up in a dull grey hallway and looked at the numbers on the doors in front of him. Ten, eight… He was going the wrong way. Ella Yeung was in room sixteen, so he changed direction, ignoring the curious glances from people behind their glass half-walls. Twelve, fourteen…

Sixteen…

At the sound of his quick rap on her open door,

Ella turned and a long, lovely leg caught his attention. He was tempted to look for longer—and couldn't help noticing her white skirt and emerald-green sleeveless top—but he knew he had to rein in his admiration and act as professionally as possible, even if there was something about Ella Yeung that made his head spin.

With her, given what she'd recently endured, he had to be ultra-professional. Difficult when all he wanted to do was run his eyes over her...

He lifted his eyes to her face and was happy to see some colour there.

Judging from the curiosity in her still cool eyes, she'd heard that Winters and the HR guy were gone and was perhaps wondering how that had come about. She was the only person who was entitled to some answers.

'Can I come in?' he asked, after greeting her.

'Sure,' she replied, gesturing him inside her office. She walked past him to sit on the edge of her desk. He wasn't invited to take a seat, he noticed.

Micah looked around her space and noticed the stack of dusty boxes in the corner, some old chairs and two broken filing cabinets. A laptop rested on the surface of a scarred wooden desk.

He'd learned a lot about Ella Yeung over the past forty-eight hours and the thought of her being banished to this dreadful office, wasting her considerable talent, annoyed him. Thank God Winters was gone or else he'd have fired him just for that.

'I thought I'd give you a personal update on the changes here,' he said, sliding his hands into the pockets of his trousers. Hands that wanted to touch her hips and her butt, hands that wanted to cradle her face, cup her breast. Of all the women in the world, he had the luck to be fiercely attracted to someone who was completely, solidly off-limits.

He'd heard the emotion in her voice the day before yesterday when she'd recounted her awful experience but he'd been impressed by her strength and admired her determination to stop Pillay's reprehensible actions. Ella Yeung had hidden depths...

Depths that would remain unexplored.

'The office gossip has been working overtime,' Ella replied. 'They're saying that Ben took early retirement, but I suspect you fired him.'

'I did.' And he'd do it a hundred times over. During the man's exit interview, Micah had ascertained that Winters was a raging misogynist. When he'd suggested that Ella had 'asked for Pillay's attention', Micah had nearly lost it. Micah refused to condone his repulsive world view by allowing him to take early retirement instead of having his employment terminated.

He'd also fired their Director of Human Resources, and the Le Roux Events Human Resources officer, as he told Ella.

Ella nodded, folded her arms and tapped her fingernail against her bicep. 'Thank you.'

He shook his head. 'It was the right thing to do. I'm just sorry it took so long for this to be resolved. We will be placing a temporary manager in Winters' place and, should you wish to resume work at your old position, we'd be grateful to have you,' Micah added. 'You'd return to a hefty pay rise and better perks.

'I've done my research, talked to some of your clients, suppliers and your colleagues. You work hard and you are damn good at what you do. The salary increase is what other event planners of your experience earn. I'm sorry to tell you that equal pay for equal jobs was another one of our policies that Winters did not follow.'

Ella grimaced. 'That doesn't surprise me.'

'We're overhauling this company and we will be making big changes. We'd like you to be a part of that.'

'Have you fired Pillay as a client?' Ella demanded.

He grimaced. 'I want to, and so does my brother, but our lawyers want us to hold off until we gather more evidence. I've hired a private detective to track down other women he's harassed—'

'I can give you some names of women who left the company because of him,' Ella said, interrupting him.

Micah nodded. 'That would be great. If my PI can get them to make a statement, we'll add their experiences to the case we are building against him.'

'Intellectually I understand that, but my word should be enough.' Ella's voice shook with anger.

He wanted to touch her, to pull her into him to offer her some comfort, but knew he shouldn't. However, he couldn't resist taking her hand and squeezing gently before releasing her quickly. 'It absolutely should be but, unfortunately, it isn't. I want to nail him, Ella, I really do, but we need to be patient just for a little longer.'

She stared at him, her unusual brown eyes bright with frustration. He knew she wanted to argue, to protest, and was grateful when she took a deep breath and nodded. 'I'm in the process of moving to the UK and plan to fly out a couple of days after I finish working out my notice here. If he hasn't been fired as a client by that time, I will not consider returning to work here. And, once I get on that plane, I'm not coming back.'

She'd put him on notice as well. Good thing that he worked well under pressure because he had no intention of losing her. Losing her *skill set*, he corrected himself... Good people were hard to find.

Her eyes dropped and he followed her gaze, surprised she was looking at his hands. What was she thinking? Could it be she wanted him to touch her? A fireball of lust skittered up his arm and fired its way down his spinal cord. It took all of his willpower to keep his expression implacable, to casually drop his hands when all he wanted was her sexy mouth under his, his hands on her slim body.

Or, and much more likely, she was wondering why the hell he was touching her—an employee, and someone who'd recently received unwanted male attention. Was he insane? What was he thinking?

He clenched his fist. 'I'm sorry, I shouldn't have touched you.'

Ella shook her head. 'It's fine...um... I know you were just trying to reassure me.'

Reassurance...sure. Let her think that. She certainly didn't need to know that he'd been slammed by the most intense sexual attraction he'd ever experienced in his life. No big deal.

Feeling hot, he looked around for the remote control to the air-conditioner. Finding it on that credenza, he picked it up and realised that this wasn't his space—

well, technically it was, but it was *her* office—so he asked her if he could drop the temperature in the room.

She agreed and Micah put it on cold and high, and then, remembering Ella's sleeveless top, settled on a temperature they could both live with. Tossing the remote control on her desk, he pulled up two old office chairs and gestured for her to sit. He sat opposite her and leaned back in his chair, linking his hands across his stomach. He casually lifted his ankle to rest it on his bended knee.

Now came the difficult bit... But he was the company trouble-shooter and it was his job to sort out problems. And, in Ella's case, that was finding out whether she intended to sue Le Roux International or not. She had a case, and she deserved some sort of compensation, which he was happy to pay her, but he'd like to avoid the enormous legal bills.

He could try and tease the answer from her but he was exhausted and decided on a direct approach. 'Look, Ella, we both know that if you wanted to you could sue my company, and we'd end up paying you a large settlement because of how badly this was handled. Do you intend to do that?'

She nodded. 'I've thought about it but I haven't made up my mind yet.'

Fair enough.

Ella stared at a point behind his head. 'Your offer for me to return to work—provided Pillay is no longer a client—is tempting. I love my job. But I couldn't work for a company I'm suing. That would be, well, uncomfortable. And, if I emigrate, I do want to leave all this behind me.'

Micah thought this was a perfect chance to segue into making her an alternative offer. One that would provide her with a serious amount of cash without going through the legal system. A solution that would also give him the help he so desperately needed.

Micah pushed his hand through his hair and then tapped the wooden surface of her desk, his fingertips moving at a rapid beat. He saw Ella look down and, when she cocked her head to the side, he clenched his fist. He only ever tapped his fingers when he was nervous and, for goodness' sake, there was really no reason to be nervous.

'How would you like to spend the next three weeks doing something other than twiddling your thumbs?' Micah asked.

Interest flickered in her eyes, along with wariness. 'And what would that be?'

Now came the tricky bit: How much to tell her? Thadie was a paparazzi's dream subject—gorgeous, lovely, rich and successful, and she was newsworthy. So far, they'd managed to keep the news of her wedding venue cancellation a secret, and they'd like to keep it that way. If the story was leaked, it would make a splash. *How had this happened? Why couldn't Le Roux organise something as simple as a wedding reception? What was happening behind the scenes?*

Thadie was one of the country's richest women and Clyde, her ex-rugby-star turned commentator fiancé, was a national hero, so the interest in them was sky-high. He needed to keep his cards close to his chest and that meant telling as few people as possible.

But keeping this a secret from someone whose help he needed was going to hamper her efforts. How could he get her cooperation as well as ensure her silence? Micah considered some strategies and discarded others, one thought tumbling over that other. He decided to tiptoe through this minefield.

'If you agree not to sue us, I'll pay you a hundred thousand pounds—we work in pounds, not rands—to do some work for me.'

Her eyebrows flew up as shock brightened her eyes. 'And what work would that be?'

'Event planning work. I need a venue on a specific day, fairly soon. If you manage to secure one, I'll pay you another hundred thousand on the proviso that nothing appears in the press about our search, the venue and us working together. If you choose not to do the work, I'll still pay you the first instalment to compensate you for how badly you were treated at Le Roux Events. I know that money can't change what happened but...' He shrugged. 'Unfortunately money is all we can offer.'

Ella tipped her head to the side and looked at him, intrigued. 'We both know that any lawyer I hired would demand more.'

Money was no object. 'Then hit me with a figure,' he suggested.

She took a couple of minutes, no doubt doing some mental arithmetic. He was expecting her to ask for millions and was surprised when she only asked for another hundred grand—three hundred thousand altogether. Too low, he suddenly decided, she deserved more. A lot more.

'What about two-fifty up front and another two-fifty once it's all complete?'

Her mouth dropped open and her eyes widened. 'Five hundred thousand pounds? With that sort of money, I could set up my own events planning company and maybe even buy a venue suitable for luxury events. I want to specialise in intimate family occasions, weddings, birthdays and events I like,' she explained. 'I'm good at those.'

'From what I've heard, you are good at everything you do,' Micah murmured.

She blushed, and her gaze clashed with his, but she immediately looked away. Micah sighed. Ella was trying hard to remain cool and unmoved but he knew that she was feeling anything but. He knew women, knew them well, and he'd had a lot of experience in picking up non-verbal cues when his attraction was reciprocated.

Ella liked what she saw. She wasn't being obvious about it, licking her lips or tilting her head. If anything, she was fighting her reaction to him. But the rapid beating pulse point in the side of her neck, her small, tight nipples under her shirt and the pale pink tinge to her skin gave her away.

He rubbed his hand over his jaw, mentally cursing the situation. He'd found an event planner, which was excellent news. Not so excellent was their immediate, compelling and dynamic reaction to each other.

It was just his lousy luck that the one woman who

caused him to feel like this was his employee, and the last woman he should get involved with right now. Even if that hadn't been a factor, he and Jago had a deal that they never played where they worked. Their father, Theo, had no problem sleeping with his secretaries, marketing managers, accountants and in-house lawyers. It made for some uncomfortable workplace situations, and had cost the company a bundle in lost talent over the years, because his lovers always moved on to other employers when Theo dumped them.

Over the last twenty years, Micah had trained himself to be less impulsive, more patient. To think before he spoke. Now it took all of his willpower not to lean forward and capture that sassy mouth. To discover her taste, to feel her luscious skin under his arms, to slide inside her warm heat…

Micah stood and walked to the window, forcing it open and pulling in some fresh air. He kept work and sex miles apart. Negotiating with a woman to whom he was attracted was a fresh hell, a place he hadn't visited before.

His week was just getting more and more complicated.

CHAPTER THREE

THE POSSIBILITY OF half a million pounds? Was she having an auditory hallucination?

No, Micah didn't look as though he was teasing her. Those bright blue eyes were sombre and his expression was heart-attack serious.

Ella opened her mouth to say yes, then snapped it closed and shook her head. What, was he the snake charmer and she was being hypnotised into doing what he wanted? Ridiculous!

Ella dropped her eyes and they came to rest on his strong wrist, sporting a vintage Rolex from the sixties. The watch suited his he-man, too-cool-for-school, rabble-rouser vibe. There were more hints of his rebellion; on his other wrist, he wore two bracelets, one a thick, braided leather and the other a series of alternating black and blue beads interspersed with silver. His stubble was too thick to be designer and his nose—she could tell by the bump in the otherwise straight ridge—had been broken more than once. She could see the tiny holes in his earlobe that suggested he'd once worn earrings and through the material of his shirt she caught the outline of a bold tattoo covering his right pec.

Underneath his designer threads and his CEO persona, Micah Le Roux was a rebel and the thought—and the man—made her hot.

Ella watched as he stood up and walked over to the window, the same one she'd used to watch him walk across the car park. When he'd stepped into her office earlier, he'd brought with him an electrical storm. Lightning fizzed, thunder rumbled and thunderheads whirled and swirled. She felt primal, elemental, as if she were the original Eve and she was about to taste rain for the first time. Nothing much had changed in the fifteen minutes since.

She still felt like she was surfing the bands of a hurricane. Dear Lord, what was wrong with her? Ella pulled her tongue off the roof of her mouth and looked around for a distraction. She needed time to think rationally and carefully.

Ella pushed back her chair and glanced towards her office door.

It was shut.

The door was *shut*. And she hadn't noticed. She lifted her hand to her throat and stared at the panelled door, panic climbing. She needed to get that open as soon as she could.

Bad things happened behind closed doors when she was alone with strange men.

Ella stood abruptly and moved towards the door. She felt his eyes on her back as she opened it wide before picking up a box and wedging it in front of the door so that it couldn't blow shut.

He pushed his hand into his hair, looking uncomfortable. His eyes bounced between the open door and her, his expression thoughtful. Then he surprised her by picking up the bottle of water that sat on her desk and twisting the cap open before handing it to her.

Who *was* this man?

Ella sipped her water, hoping that her pulse would soon drop to not-about-to-have-a-panic-attack levels. Her anxiety receded and her breath evened out but her heart was still skipping around her chest, acting as if she'd never seen a good-looking guy before.

The truth was she'd never met anyone like Micah Le Roux, who was both straightforward and, seemingly, sensitive. And had she mentioned sexy?

Do try to focus on what is important, Ella.

Ella rolled her shoulders, intrigued despite herself about his offer. She'd told him a little white lie earlier; she'd never seriously considered suing Le Roux International. Mostly because it sounded expensive but also because, as she'd said, she did want to put these last few months behind her.

But if Micah was willing to compensate her, provided she find him a venue, she'd be a fool to turn down his offer. Especially since it would give her the capital to start her own business…

'Okay, so you want me to find you a particular venue on a particular date and you're prepared to pay me a lot of money to do that. What's the catch?'

Micah's expression hardened. 'It's imperative that

you do not leak any information about the venue, the function or anything we discuss.'

Ella felt her skin shrink, feeling like a caterpillar encased in a too-tight cocoon. She prided herself on her integrity and she'd never, ever let slip a detail about any function. And she now knew, personally, what it felt like to be the subject of office gossip and speculation.

'I'm not going to say anything, Mr Le Roux. You either believe me or you don't.' She wasn't going to beg him to. She'd done that before, both times with far more at stake than five hundred thousand pounds. She couldn't put a price on her mum's death or being pushed out of her job. From this moment on, people either believed her or they didn't; she wasn't going to beg them to.

After a brief pause, Micah explained how his sister had lost her wedding venue and that she and her wedding planner—Anna de Palmer-Whyte, wedding planner to the rich and famous—hadn't managed to secure another venue. Ella was outraged by what had happened and felt awful for Thadie Le Roux for losing her booking at the utterly lovely venue. It was a favourite amongst the elite of the country, and for good reason. It was a fairy-tale place with an amazing, ornate ballroom, amazing gardens and facilities. Weddings were so stressful at the best of times and to have this happen was catastrophic.

'I'm so sorry,' Ella said, genuinely upset by the news. 'Do you have any idea who could've done something so horrible?'

Micah shook his head, looking thunderous. 'God

help him if I find him.' He pushed his hand through his curls. 'The important thing is to find Thadie a venue.'

Ella frowned, confused. 'So, you are wanting to pay me a lot of money for me to spend a few days looking at suitable venues in and around Johannesburg, checking whether they are available and arranging for you to visit them? But isn't that something Anna should be doing? And, if she is doing that, and I'm pretty sure she is, why would you hire me to duplicate her efforts?'

His eyes turned darker, bluer. If that was at all possible. 'Anna hasn't been able to find anything yet, so I suggested that we extend our search. If you agree, we will visit various venues outside of the city...together. The Drakensberg, Clarens, the Midlands. We might fly to some, drive to others. If we find any venues suitable, I'll pay to secure the date, and at the end we'll narrow it down to three. Then we will visit them again, this time with Thadie and Anna, who will make the final decision.'

He wasn't playing around, Ella thought. He expected her to spend long hours, in cars, planes and confined spaces, with a stranger. She couldn't do it. Not even for half a million pounds. God, she couldn't even be in a room with a closed door with him, some place where there were colleagues down the hall.

You were fine with the closed door until your brain kicked in and told you that you should be feeling scared. Up until then, you were fine being alone with him... Why can't you trust yourself any more? Trust your gut?

Ella ignored her inner voice and waved it away. Her

gut was unreliable, so she intended to be sensible and to err on the side of caution.

Sure, the money would be nice—very nice indeed—and she desperately wanted to do something besides sitting in this office but…she couldn't.

It was too much of a risk.

'You'll be staying in five-star accommodation, flying on luxury planes or driving my brand-new Bentayga—'

'I'll be driving it?' Ella asked, surprised.

'I'll need to work occasionally so, yeah, I'd expect you to drive,' Micah said.

Wow. To her, driving his fantastic car was a perk. And, judging by his small smile, he knew it.

'You'll be eating excellent food and drinking great wine,' Micah continued, ignoring her interruption. 'You'll be out of this dismal office and seeing some beautiful parts of the country.'

Except that she'd be alone, for an extended time, with a stranger.

God, she was tempted, so tempted. She was ninety-five per cent sure that she'd be safe with Micah, that nothing would happen that she didn't want to—nothing would happen, full-stop!—but that damn five per cent of uncertainty held her by the throat and wouldn't let her go.

But that wasn't the *only* reason she was hesitant to take him up on his offer. Honesty had her admitting that another part of her *wanted* something to happen between them.

The truth was that she was startlingly, crazily attracted to Micah. She wanted to step into his arms, nuzzle her nose into his neck and pull his shirt from those dark, smart designer jeans. After being groped by Pillay, she didn't think she'd ever feel lust again, but here she was, wondering whether he tasted as good as he looked, whether his muscle had muscles and whether he had those sexy hip muscles she so loved on men. She wanted him, harder and hotter than anything she'd experienced before. She didn't know how to handle feeling so off-kilter, unbalanced, so thoroughly, crazily turned on.

And what if something happened, something she asked for, and at the last minute, she freaked out? What would he think of her? How would they work together after that? No, it was easier, safer, to walk away, so that was what she'd do.

She would still receive two hundred and fifty thousand pounds, a cracking amount, but she had to protect herself in every way possible.

Forcing herself to meet his eyes, she twisted her lips. 'Sorry, but I'm not the right person for this job.'

Ella saw the frustration in his eyes, and a little bit of panic, and realised how important it was for him to solve this problem for his sister. In fact, it was a lovely thing for him to do, but she couldn't let that sway her. She had to protect herself, and that meant not putting herself in positions that could backfire. He was asking her to be alone with him for long stretches of time, to stay overnight at venues out of the city, and her comfort zone. He was a fit, strong guy and she wouldn't have a chance in hell against him. While she was reasonably sure that he was one of the good guys, she couldn't take that chance.

Ella was about to refuse again when his phone rang, breaking their tense silence. Micah jerked the device out of his trousers pocket and scowled down at the screen. She watched as tenderness replaced anxiety, affection chased away frustration. He held up his finger, silently asking her to wait, and answered his video call.

'Hey, how are my two favourite guys?'

'Hi, Unca Micah.' A very young, piping voice drifted over to Ella. Unable to resist, she craned her neck to see the source of the high pitched voice. Instead of the one child she'd expected, she saw two, both with bright blue eyes, lovely light-brown skin and curly hair. They wore different coloured T-shirts and shorts but it was obvious they were twins.

'Why aren't you guys smiling?' Micah asked, sitting on the edge of the desk. 'Did Mummy send you to the naughty corner again?'

'Mmm-hmm.'

Ella watched, fascinated by the half-smile that caused Micah's lips to twitch. His eyes, lighter and brighter, were full of amusement and he looked years younger. When he did it properly, Ella was fairly sure his smile could blister paint.

'We said dammit and Mummy put us in the naughty corner for five minutes!'

Micah swallowed and Ella suspected he was biting the inside of his cheek to keep his expression sober. 'Guys, that's a bad word. You shouldn't say it,' Micah told them, his voice serious.

Their response was quick and hot. 'Then why don't you go to the naughty corner, because you say it all the time!'

'It's not fair!' the other twin added.

Ella slapped her hand over her mouth to stop herself from laughing. 'You're right, I should go to the naughty corner, maybe even for *fifteen* minutes.'

'But that's for ever!'

Micah nodded, his expression still serious. 'Don't repeat my bad words, guys, and listen to your mum. I've got to go but I'll talk to you guys later.'

He disconnected the call and gently banged the face of his phone against his forehead.

'Ugh, my sister is going to tear a strip off me again,' he told her, finally allowing his smile to bloom. It creased the corner of his eyes, showed off his white, even teeth and dropped another few years off his face. Ella glanced at the wall, disappointed when she didn't see the paint bubbling.

'I think they won that round,' she pointed out, unable to resist teasing him just a little.

'I do try to watch my language around them but I'm not always successful.'

Ella was surprised Johannesburg's favourite bachelor billionaire had even taken their call—which had to have been authorised by their mum, so she couldn't be too mad at her brother—and was also shocked he sounded so at ease with the twins. It was obvious that he spent a lot of time with them and spoke to them often.

He was smart, nice to kids and far too attractive,

Ella thought, and she needed to leave his presence before she did something stupid and agreed to spend three
weeks with him hunting down a venue.

It took a lot of effort for her to stand up and hold
out her hand. 'I'll take the two hundred and fifty thousand but I'll pass on your other offer. Anna de Palmer-
Whyte is amazing; I'm sure she'll find you a venue.'

Ella turned and hurried towards the door, knowing that if she stayed, if he smiled, she might just say
yes. And that wasn't something she could afford to do.

She definitely couldn't return to her old job at Le Roux
Events, Ella decided at the end of what had been a long,
interesting, weird day. And, with the quarter million
pounds Micah had promised to pay her as a settlement,
she could take some time to decide what she really
wanted to do, where she wanted to be.

It gave her some breathing room but she'd still emigrate. If she was going to start a new life it might as
well be in another country, Ella thought as she headed
to her leased car on the far side of the staff car park.
The UK would be a blank slate, some place to start
afresh, to reinvent herself.

To start again…

How many more times would she have to do that?
She'd had to pick herself up after her mum's death and
grieve on her own, recover on her own. Her father had
supplied her with a place to stay and money, but he'd
stopped emotionally engaging with her, and in time
had stopped talking to her altogether. She'd spent the
past decade trying to bash through the steel plate he'd

erected around him, to no avail. She could only give him so much time, so much energy, and she was done. He didn't want her in his life so she was giving him what he wanted.

After university, she'd returned to the coastal city, found an apartment and a job and in time had received the offer from Le Roux Events, which necessitated her moving to Johannesburg, a fast-paced and cutthroat city. She'd embraced the new start and the challenge but then her world had fallen apart...

Hopefully, this third reset would be the charm.

'Seven hundred and fifty thousand pounds and nothing will happen.'

Ella jerked her head up to see Micah Le Roux leaning his butt against the door of her hatchback, its cherry-red paint glinting in the sun. Designer sunglasses shielded his eyes from the still potent late-afternoon sun and she could see the streaks of deep gold in his hair. Earlier she'd given him thirty minutes to vacate her office and then had spent the rest of the afternoon reading up on him online. She now knew his tan and streaked hair came from spending as much time as he could outside and that he spent his free weekends running triathlons, sailing or doing adventure-trail running.

He adored his family—his twin, Jago, and his much younger sister, Thadie, socialite and social media influencer, the mother of the twin boys she'd seen on his screen. According to the all-knowing Internet, he wasn't dating anyone at the moment and didn't do serious relationships. Micah Le Roux liked variety and wore his single status like a badge of honour. He liked red wine, lived in his wing of the famous, historical family mansion in Sandhurst and had been voted as one of the most influential men under forty on the continent.

And he was standing by her car, waiting for her. Ella's heart bounced around her ribcage and she felt her breathing turn shallow and her skin prickle with awareness. What was it about this man that caused her brain to stop working and her joints to liquefy? She'd dealt with many wealthy, good-looking guys but no one had made her feel so off-balance, so aware, so feminine, as Micah did.

'What do you think, Ella?' Micah asked as she used her car's remote control to unlock it. She walked past him to open the boot and tossed her bag inside, scowling at her seldom-used gym bag. His muscled, fit body was a reminder that she needed to start exercising again...

Holding her phone and her car keys in one hand, she slammed the boot lid closed and cursed when it didn't catch. She slammed it again, harder, taking some of her frustration out on the car.

Ella joined Micah by the driver's door. 'I'm not interested, Micah.' What a lie; of course she was interested. And scared.

'Except that you are.' She started to protest and stopped when he held up his hand. 'I saw it in your eyes; you want to help me. And the additional money interests you too.'

Ella wrinkled her nose. Of course it did; she wasn't a saint.

Micah leaned his hip into her car again, his eyes connecting with hers, so deep and such an incredible shade of blue.

'You're scared to be alone with me,' he murmured. 'I'm sorry it took me so long to figure that out but I got there in the end.'

Ella's head shot up at his sympathetic statement, her gaze flying across his face, trying to see if he was mocking her. No, he looked and sounded genuine.

'I need your help, Ella, but I understand why you can't trust me or the situation,' Micah softly stated. 'You have every reason to feel that way. But I *do* need your help.'

Frustration passed through his eyes. 'I don't know how to reassure you except to tell you that I'd never hurt you, or any other woman, and that you can trust me. You're my employee, and I never play where I work.'

Ella felt herself wavering, wanting to believe him. But that could be her insane attraction to him clouding her reasoning.

'I instinctively trusted you earlier, Ella, when you told me about Pillay. Can you not do the same for me?'

She considered his words. He was right. He hadn't hemmed or hawed, he'd listened and sprung into action. He hadn't changed his mind upon hearing who had accosted her, even though Pillay was part of his A-list social circle and she was sure they'd met.

Could she trust herself, trust her gut feeling that

Micah would never make an unwanted advance? Would she miss out on a huge opportunity because she was five per cent scared, maybe even less?

'I believed you. Can you do the same for me?'

Micah believing in her was huge, a balm to her battered soul. After so many defeats and disappointments, she was intensely grateful to be taken seriously.

So grateful that she could kiss him...

Ella sighed. That wasn't breaking news. She'd wanted to kiss him from the moment she laid eyes on him again a few hours ago. But kissing wasn't on the agenda, and if she accepted his offer she would be there to work, not play. Pity, she thought. In another life, at another time, if she'd been someone different—someone confident and self-assured—Micah Le Roux, she was sure, would be a fun way to pass some time.

'Well? Do you? Trust me, that is,' Micah demanded, and she heard a hint of impatience in his voice.

She did. She knew she did. Her gut had never yelled this loudly before, so she nodded. 'Yes, I do.'

'Thank God,' Micah muttered.

Ella smiled at him. 'You know, all the articles about you all mention how charismatic you are, how you can charm anyone, anywhere. I think that's true but I don't think that's who you really are. I think you are more impatient and demanding than most people realise.'

Micah's eyes widened in shock, and his mouth fell open. Then he laughed, a deep belly-laugh that raised the hair on her arms and created heat between her legs. If his smile was potent, then his laugh was dazzling and delightful on a million different levels. She wanted to dance in it, roll around in it, wrap herself up in it…

'You're right. I am all those things, and most people never suspect that. How did you?'

She didn't know how to answer his question, she just did. To her, it was as obvious as his blue eyes and his wide shoulders.

'So, knowing that, are you prepared to spend the next three weeks on and off in my company?' Micah asked her, suddenly serious.

'I am,' Ella told him. 'But can I ask you one more thing?'

Amusement flashed in his eyes. 'A million pounds is my highest offer,' he told her with an easy smile.

Ella shook her head. 'I'm not asking for more money, Micah.'

'Okay, we'll settle on seven-fifty for now, Ella. What's your question?'

Three quarters of a *million*… The mind boggled. But her request wasn't about the money. This was one last test, one more hurdle for him to jump over and, if he managed it, she knew she'd never spend another moment worrying about him. She gathered her courage. 'You keep looking at my mouth. Does that mean you want to kiss me?'

He didn't hesitate to nod. 'Yeah, of course I do,' he answered in a gruff voice.

She knew he'd say that but he hadn't dropped his head or moved closer to put his words into action. So far, so good. 'Why?' she asked, pushing him, loving his direct way of answering her question.

'Because I'm so damn attracted to you it actually hurts. I'd love to know how you feel in my arms, what you taste like, whether your skin is as soft as I think it is.'

Oh, God. His gaze darted between her mouth and eyes and she felt her back arching, her body betraying her.

'But I won't, because I gave you my word.' He lifted his hand, as if to touch her mouth or cheek, but dropped it before he could make contact with her skin. She was both relieved and disappointed. Relieved because he'd kept his word, disappointed because she wanted nothing more than to kiss him. 'You said that you keep your word. I do, too.'

Micah reached past her to open her car door and, when he spoke again, his tone was brisk and businesslike. 'I'd like you to spend the day tomorrow researching possible venues in areas not too far from here. I'm thinking Clarens, Parys—places like that. If you find any options, set up appointments for tomorrow and we'll drive down.'

Her mind was spinning but she managed to nod.

'I'll confirm a pick-up time with you tomorrow, but it'll be early.'

'I'm not good at early,' Ella confessed, sliding behind the wheel of her car. 'If you give me your number, I'll send you a GPS pin for my address.'

He asked for her number, punched it into his phone and a few seconds later her phone rang. 'That's my private number—save it.'

Oh, and he was bossy too! Ella resisted the urge to salute.

Micah closed her door and bent down so that their heads were level. 'We'll talk tomorrow, Ella.'

She nodded and cranked the key to start her car. She turned her head to look into Micah's eyes and couldn't help her gaze dropping to his sexy mouth. She sighed and, when she lifted her eyes again, saw amused frustration on his face.

He sighed. 'It's going to be a long, long three weeks, isn't it? Because you want to kiss me as much as I do you.'

He was so honest, and she liked it. She was also so busted. 'Yes, but we're adults. We'll cope.'

'Speak for yourself,' Micah muttered before walking away.

She grinned at his broad back and shook her head. He was the only person she knew who could be both charming and grumpy. She rather liked it. She liked him.

He was right, she thought as she drove away, it was going to be a very long three weeks.

CHAPTER FOUR

MICAH PARKED THE Bentayga in his parking bay within the Hadleigh House garage and lifted his hands, noticing his trembling fingers. He switched off the ignition and leaned forward, placing his head on his custom-leather steering wheel. On the way home, a forty-five-minute drive, he'd ducked in and out of traffic, his entire concentration on the road and Johannesburg's crazy drivers. But, now that he was home, he couldn't avoid thinking of Ella.

He hadn't had this strong a reaction to a woman in what seemed like a hundred years. Or, frankly, ever. From the moment he'd laid eyes on her, he'd imagined her head on his pillow, her naked body on his white sheets. He wanted her in the worst way and couldn't work out why. She was lovely, but more wholesome than glamorous, more down to earth than fabulous. Because he was as shallow as a puddle, and he liked being that way when it came to relationships, he wasn't normally attracted to anyone who wasn't glamourous and over-the-top fabulous.

He desperately wanted to take Ella to bed and do

wicked, wonderful things to her while he had her in it. But he'd made her a promise and he intended to keep it—keeping his word was vitally important to him. He'd be a monk around her. A frustrated monk, but a monk none the less.

Micah looked around the detached eight-car garage they shared with his stepmother, Liyana. His 1967 Jaguar E-type was covered with its custom-made tarpaulin and the fabric was covered in a thin layer of dust. He hadn't driven it for months. Then again, neither had he taken his Ducati out for a spin either. He couldn't remember when last he'd used the speedboat he shared with Jago, and it had been even longer since they'd taken the jet skis out on the water. There were ATVs and dirt bikes, and none of them had been touched in years.

They had too many toys and too little time, too much work to do.

Micah saw that Jago's car was gone. He glanced towards Liyana's end of the garage and noticed that both her cars were in residence, which meant that Liyana was…somewhere. London? Milan? It was hard to keep up with his stepmother, not that he wanted to.

He and Liyana had what could be described at best as a frosty relationship, and at worst as a long-standing cold war from the moment they'd met when he'd been nine, just a few weeks after his mum's death. The next nine years had been a raging battle between them. The two years after Brianna's accident had been filled with silence, and these days they didn't talk more than they had to. Too much had happened and she'd hurled too many acid-tipped accusations at him.

'Brianna's condition is your fault.'

'You are a bad influence on Thadie and I should keep you away from her.'

'You don't deserve to be part of this family after what you did.'

Leaving the garage, Micah headed to the house but made a detour to a wooden bench at the base of one of the oldest oak trees on the property, where he sat and rested his forearms on his knees, childhood memories rolling over him. In the space of a couple of months, he'd lost his mum, acquired a stepmum, seen the family house stripped of his mother's possessions and been told that it was time for a new start, a new chapter. Within a year, he'd also acquired a half-sister, and it had been too much to deal with. He'd been upset, grief-stricken, confused and angry, and he'd acted out...

He'd been an absolute terror, obstreperous and defiant, rebellious and lost. He'd pulled Jago into pranks, some of which had been downright dangerous. He looked at the two-storey-high roof of the garage and his blood iced at the memory of the two of them sliding down the roof and off its edge to land on a stack of mattresses on the grass below. He could've broken a leg, Jago could've broken his spine... If the twins even thought about doing something like that in the future, he'd ground them for life!

But back then he hadn't cared, he'd just been looking for trouble, for attention good or bad. His relationship with his father, when he was around, was terrible.

Unlike his siblings and his late mother, Micah didn't hesitate to call his father out for acting like a jerk, something Theo excelled at—and, when she wasn't yelling at him for being impulsive, reckless or for doing something stupid, Liyana ignored him. Jabu, their family butler, had been more of a parent than his father and stepmother put together.

It had all come to a head a month or two after his eighteenth birthday. He'd been on his own at Hadleigh House—Jago had been away on a rugby tour and Micah had been suspended from school for the third time that year. He had been rubbing on his father's and Liyana's last nerve...deliberately, he was sure. His father, he of the volatile temper, had started yelling at Liyana and him. Then Theo had focused all of his ire on Micah and their argument had rapidly escalated. Theo had pushed him and he'd pushed back. Then Theo had thrown a punch, his fist breaking Micah's nose and spilling his blood on the ancient Persian carpet. Despite being constantly at loggerheads, he'd never imagined, not once, that his father would physically hurt him.

Shocked, stunned, emotionally eviscerated, the physical pain had been secondary, almost an afterthought. Knowing he had to leave, he'd stormed out of the house and, out of habit, called Brianna.

While Jago never hesitated to call him out, Brianna had always, *always* agreed with him and taken his side. He'd told her what had happened and that he planned to get drunk and stoned. She'd begged him not to go, told him that the bar he intended to visit was in a dangerous area and that he might get hurt. He'd brushed her off, never thinking that she'd follow him to that bad area of town, and had proceeded to get drunk, then high. When he'd finally made it home the next morning—he had vague memories of an older blonde who'd taken him home and into her bed—he'd been met by his father and Liyana, red-eyed and weeping.

Brianna had been in a head-on car accident, he'd been told, had massive head injuries and was on life support. Nobody had understood why she'd been out at night, why she'd been in that area of town. Her parents then accessed her mobile phone and they'd quickly established, by the numerous voice messages she'd sent Micah, that she'd been worried about him, upset that he hadn't returned her calls or messages. Her last message had been that she was going to look for him. Not used to driving at night, she'd lost control of her zippy car and had veered into the oncoming lane…

Brianna had eventually been moved off life support and onto a feeding tube and she had been moved to a private long-term-care medical facility. To this day she remained in a profound state of unconsciousness, had minimal brain activity and her prognosis for recovery was slim to none. Yet her parents continued to hold out hope that, with the field of neuroscience advancing rapidly, someone, somewhere, would find a way to bring their only child back to them. And her parents had never stopped blaming Micah for her condition.

That was okay, because he blamed himself too.

His first year at university had been a blur, a lost time period of bouncing between lectures, lawyers and sessions with a psychologist to help him deal with his guilt and grief. After the court case had been dismissed—he'd not been found *legally* liable for her injuries—he'd slowly started to turn over a new leaf. It had taken time, but he'd managed to get his temper under control and learned how to think before reacting. He'd also made a couple of vows to himself—most importantly that he'd never again be a source of pain for anyone he loved and cared about. That meant never putting himself in a situation where he risked hurting anyone, especially a woman, again.

It was simple: if Brianna could never have her greatest wish fulfilled—to have a family and kids—then neither could he.

Micah heard a familiar clearing of a throat and looked up to see Jabu standing on the path, his hands linked behind his back. His face radiated dignity, and within his dark eyes Micah read his concern.

'*Sawubona*, Mkulu,' he said, greeting him in Zulu, and using the word for 'grandfather'. It was also a word used for elderly men held in high regard, which Micah did.

Jabu lifted his grey eyebrows. 'As a child, when you were upset I could usually find you up this tree. Is everything all right?'

Micah stood up and walked over to the shorter man, gently gripping his shoulder. He knew Jabu worried about him and, since he'd caused the man enough grief, he forced a smile. 'Everything is fine, Mkulu.'

Jabu sent him a disbelieving look.

'Your stepmother is asking for a report. She wants to know if you've made any progress on finding a wedding venue,' Jabu stated as they walked to the side entrance of Hadleigh House. Instead of using the massive front hall, with its hand-carved double-wide staircase and impressive paintings, he and his twin accessed their suites via a back staircase. Jabu punched in the code to open the door and Micah stepped back to allow him into the house first.

Did Liyana honestly think he could magic a venue out of thin air? Before he could reply, Jabu spoke again. 'I told her that you are working on it and that I'm sure you'll find something soon.'

'Thank you. If she asks again, tell her that I have help and that I am on it.' He and Liyana had been passing messages to each other for twenty years through Jabu and he'd never once complained. It was childish and immature but it was also a habit that kept the peace. Life was better for all of them when he and Liyana ignored each other as much as possible.

'I had another job offer today,' Jabu told him, pulling a drooping rose from the vase on the hall table.

Micah, about to run up the stairs, stopped and turned to face his favourite person. He was reasonably sure Jabu would never leave them, and that he used his status of being the most headhunted butler in the country as a means of manipulating Jago and him to settle down and start families.

Micah, knowing the drill, just waited in silence.

'The family has three young boys under the age of ten. They entertain a lot, both here and at their home in Switzerland. The couple seems to be very happily married but busy; they need help.'

Translation: neither you nor Jago has provided me with grandchildren, you don't entertain enough and you need a woman in your life. 'Jabu, come on…'

Uneasiness flashed through Jabu's eyes. 'I don't earn the enormous salary you pay me, Micah.'

Ah, so he was worried about that again. It was a subject that, along with their single status, raised its head occasionally. He and Jago travelled a lot and when they were at home they were very self-sufficient. These days, Jabu's duties were limited, and they knew he felt guilty about living in the large apartment above the garage, his huge salary and the use of a company car.

'Mkulu, I know that my father never paid you what you were due when we were kids; he was a notorious skinflint and you earned the bare minimum. Jago and me—mostly me—were terrors, Theo was volatile and Liyana was demanding. You dealt with all of us without a word of complaint and with incredible dignity. Jago and I agree that you've earned an easy semi-retirement.'

'But—'

'Got to go,' Micah said, running up the stairs. On the landing, he looked down to see Jabu still standing in the hall, his eyes on a black-and-white photograph of Jago, Thadie and himself. Jabu straightened the photograph, nodded once and touched the edge of the frame with his fingertips.

Crisis, Micah thought, averted. But if Jabu was feeling restless then he'd ask Thadie to request his help with the twins for a day or two. He'd come back exhausted after running after those bundles of energy,

and his requests for a busier Hadleigh House would
die down for a month or two.

He loved Jabu, but his own children running round
the rooms of this old house would never happen.

The next day, Ella stood on a wooden deck of The Gate
boutique hotel, entranced by the sandstone cliffs of the
Golden Gate National Park. The multi layers of the cliff
and outcrops fascinated her, with each layer sporting a
different colour ranging from black to gold, to red, to
orange and ochre. She remembered visiting this area
as a child and wondered why she hadn't been back to
the park since then or visited the quaint and artistic
town on its doorstep, Clarens.

It was only a three-and-a-half-hour road trip from
Johannesburg and they'd left the city at eight that morning. She'd waited for Micah on the pavement outside
her apartment block and he'd swung his expensive car
into a parking spot a few feet from her. He'd tossed her
small suitcase into the boot of the car, handed her the
keys and told her he needed to work.

While she drove his car through the city's traffic
and onto highway, busy with trucks and empty of cars,
he'd spent the next three hours and twenty minutes on
his phone and laptop, frequently both at once. It was
only when they'd approached Clarens that he raised
his head, closed his laptop and looked around. The
on-board navigation system instructed her to bypass
the town and head for the Golden Gate National Park,
and they turned to the right not far from the towering
cliffs and the park's entrance.

This was their first appointment; they had another this afternoon and one tomorrow morning. They'd toured the grounds of the hotel, looked at the sweet chapel, inspected the kitchens and the function rooms and peeked in on the bride and groom and honeymoon suites. Micah, surprisingly, allowed her to take the lead on questioning the functions manager, and she'd covered all aspects of staging a huge event without letting the owner know she was looking for a wedding venue. Ella looked back into the function room, saw Micah shake the manager's hand and sighed at the hopeful look on the guy's face. A Le Roux function would put this place on the map and would be a stunning advertisement for the hotel. Unfortunately, she couldn't recommend it as an option for his sister's wedding.

Micah stepped onto the deck, closed the glass door behind him and joined Ella at the railing, holding two bottles of water in his hand. He opened one for her, handed it over and took a long sip. When he lowered the bottle, he sent her an easy grin. 'Hi,' he said softly.

'Hi back,' she replied equally softly, leaning her forearms on the railing, enjoying the mild breeze coming off the mountains. 'God, it's beautiful here.'

Micah nodded. 'I love this area. It's one of my favourite places to do trail runs and hike.'

'It could be one of my favourite places to sit on a deck like this and read a book,' Ella told him, smiling.

'I like to be busy,' Micah told her. That wasn't news to Ella, as he hadn't taken a breath for the entire trip from the city, either taking calls, giving orders or banging away on his laptop or phone. She hadn't minded being ignored. She'd needed the time to think.

When he'd collected her this morning, he'd acted cool and professional and she hadn't picked up a hint of the attraction she'd seen yesterday. Ella turned over his words about him being attracted to her, wanting her in his arms. Had he meant them or was he just being kind? Had he changed his mind about finding her attractive?

Maybe his attraction was a one-off, one-day thing, a soap bubble hitting a thorn or a piece of spun sugar. There one moment, gone the next. The problem was that his attraction to her might've faded, but hers was still raging.

Ella placed her tablet onto the glass-and-wood table to her right. She caught Micah looking at it and tipped her head to the side. 'What?'

'Are you sure you've got enough space on that to hold all your notes?'

She blushed a little, knowing that her habit of taking down reams of notes, most of them probably a bit unnecessary, was a source of amusement to her work colleagues. 'I don't like to miss anything.'

'Ella, you nearly wrote the equivalent of Proust's *In Search of Lost Time* in two hours.'

She didn't get the reference so she asked him to explain. 'It's supposedly the longest book in the world,' he said.

'Ha-ha, funny,' she said, but her tone lacked heat. 'It's important to me that I don't miss any details, because you never know when a little detail might be important.'

Micah rested a hip on the table and his forearm on his thigh. He was dressed casually today in a pair of tailored blue Chambray shorts—almost the same colour as the sky above—a cream button-down shirt with its sleeves rolled back and a pair of trendy trainers. 'There's a story there. Will you tell me?'

It was such a direct question, no hesitating, fudging or judgement, so she shrugged. 'I lost my mum when I was sixteen and my life became a little chaotic. Order became very important to me. I like making notes and lists.'

'They make you feel safe, in control,' Micah observed.

She nodded, surprised at his perception. 'Yes.'

'You enjoy planning events, don't you?'

Ella leaned back against the railing and looked up into his face, noticing the fine lines around his eyes, no doubt from squinting in the sun, just as he was doing now. As if he heard her thoughts, Micah dropped his sunglasses from the top of his head and covered his eyes.

He didn't give her a chance to answer. 'I was watching you and you dove into the meeting, completely confident. You asked him a dozen questions I would never have thought about.'

'Well, it's what I do,' she pointed out, though pleased at the compliment. 'And, yes, I do love it.'

He leaned his forearms on the railing and looked at the scenery, watching three vultures lazily riding the thermal bands high above them. Standing in the sun, enjoying the quiet and the cool breeze, Ella could easily pretend they were on holiday, taking a mini-break, lovers instead of work colleagues. She wanted to step between his legs, lean her head on his chest and feel his arms around her. Taking the moment, being together in the present.

But that was impossible.

'So, what do you think?' Ella asked him, reluctantly turning her attention back to the venue. It was a pretty place, built from local stone, and the interior was exquisitely decorated. There was ample accommodation in the village and surrounding areas to accommodate the wedding guests but, sadly, the place was too small. The guests would be jammed into the venue like sardines in a can. And when a wedding was so upmarket and luxurious, space to move, dance and socialise— to see and be seen—was high on the list of priorities.

Ella still believed that Johannesburg was the right place to hold the wedding and was convinced that there had to be a private estate, a museum, a vintage hall or an industrial warehouse that could be prettied up. They just needed to think outside the box.

'Very pretty.'

Ella turned at his low, intense voice, and when her eyes connected with his she immediately realised that he wasn't looking at the view or the buildings but at her, his eyes hidden by his designer sunglasses.

'I like your dress,' Micah added in his still-business-like voice. She'd wanted to look professional but to be comfortable too, so she'd chosen to wear a graphic printed white-and-brown Boho-inspired maxi dress, its halter neck leaving her arms bare.

'Thank you,' Ella replied, feeling a little at sea. He was saying the right words, but she still couldn't read him, and it was frustrating as hell.

She should stop this going-nowhere conversation, change the subject herself, but instead she dropped her gaze and idly noted that his beard was slighter thicker than it had been the day before and that his lower lip was fuller than his top lip. She wondered if he'd taste like the coffee he'd drunk earlier, or the apple he'd crunched as a mid-morning snack. Or a combination of both. She shouldn't be thinking of kissing him; he was her boss. She was advising him on a venue, trying to help him solve a pretty big problem...

But how could she concentrate when all she wanted was to be in his arms, to have his mouth on hers?

'Dammit.'

'Problem?' Micah asked and Ella cursed herself. Why did she let the mild curse leave her lips?

'No, I'm fine.'

He pulled off his sunglasses and hooked them in the vee of his shirt. 'Are you worried about being alone with me?'

God, no! Was that what he was thinking? Of course she wasn't! 'No, I'm not worried about you making a move on me.'

His mouth lifted at the corners in a sexy smirk. 'Then are you worried that *you* are going to make a move on *me*?'

Yes.

'No, of course not!' Ella scoffed, cursing her higher-than-normal voice. How did he know that? He slid his hands into the front pockets of his shorts and rested his hip against the wooden railing, his raised eyebrows silently calling her out on her lie.

'I think you want to kiss me but then you remembered that you are working for me, that we have a job to do,' he said, a hint of teasing in his voice.

Ella felt embarrassed that he could read her so easily. Why couldn't she play it cool, hide her feelings, be a little less transparent, dammit?

'We are allowed to be attracted to each other, Ella,' Micah pointed out in a reasonable tone.

Ella rubbed her forehead with her fingertips. 'Yes, I'm more attracted to you than you are to me. Happy now?' she asked, sounding belligerent.

Oh, why couldn't she keep her mouth shut? What was wrong with her?

'You think that I'm not as attracted to you as you are to me?' Micah demanded, genuinely astounded. 'Why would you think that?'

'Teasing voice, charming attitude, shuttered eyes… take your pick,' Ella replied.

His eyes caught hers and he allowed her—of that she had no doubt—to see the turmoil inside him, his hot desire, his burning need. Where did all that heat come from, and how did he manage to hide it so well?

Was charm a cloak he pulled on, one that shielded his emotions from the world? He had a reputation for being laid back and easy going, but she'd seen his irritation and impatience the other day. Was he just very adept at hiding his feelings? Maybe. Possibly.

'Did you not hear what I said yesterday about how much I want to kiss you?'

Ella dragged the toe of her shoe along a wooden beam of the deck. 'I thought you changed your mind, that it was a blip,' she admitted.

'A blip?'

'Um… Well, you were super-business-like when you picked me up, and you didn't say two words to me for more than three hours. I thought…'

'You think far too much, Ella,' Micah stated, pushing his hand through his hair.

'And you hide your thoughts too well, Micah,' Ella shot back.

'*Touché.*' Micah nodded. 'But understand this… nothing has changed. I still want you in every way a man wants a woman.'

Oh…right. Wow. That was pretty clear.

'But *I* can't make the first move here, *I* can't do a damn thing,' Micah said, his voice sounding strangled. 'My hands are tied because you work for me and *I* promised you—*promised* you!—that you were safe with me.'

He'd put a lot of emphasis on the 'I'…

'I've already resigned from your company, and I've decided that I'm not coming back to work at Le Roux Events, so I'll be leaving your employ in a little under three weeks. Does that make a difference?' Ella asked him, surprised at her question. She wasn't normally this brave. Correction: she was *never* this brave when it came to men.

He stared at her, his hands bunched in his pockets, his eyes holding hers captive.

'And what if I told you that I do feel safe with you, and I appreciate you making me feel that way? Most men would take my statements as a green light and would've been kissing me by now, trying for more.'

His eyes blazed but his stance didn't change. 'I'll say it again and I'll keep saying it: I don't force myself on women, ever.'

God, how was she supposed to resist him, fight against the rush of need and want? 'What if I kissed you? What if I placed my hands on your body, my lips on your mouth?'

The air shimmered between them, and it was as if lightning was striking all around them from the cloud-less blue sky. 'You talk far too damn much, El,' he muttered.

Ella stepped closer to him, feeling mighty, potent and, best of all, in control. Something she hadn't felt for months. She placed her hand on his muscled chest, stood on her tiptoes and did what she'd been longing to from the moment she'd first seen him—and that was to place her nose in the space where his jaw and throat met. She inhaled his scent, cologne, soap and hot male skin, and her stomach rolled over. Cupping her hand around his neck, she noticed that his hands were still bunched in his pockets and his heart was pounding. He wanted her...

She knew that as she knew her own name.

Ella placed her lips on his and nibbled and licked her tongue across his bottom lip. He was stiff, tightly coiled, and she pulled back a little to look up into his fire-blue, narrowed eyes. 'Please kiss me, Micah.'

For a moment she thought that he was going to refuse, to reject her, but then one hand was on her lower back, pulling her into his body, and the fingers of his other hand held her jaw, gently but possessively. She expected him to cover her mouth with his, to drop them into a hot, deep, slide of a kiss, but surprisingly his mouth travelled from the side of her mouth, up her cheek and back down along her jaw. When he finally returned to her lips, he nibbled, then sucked, tracing his tongue over her bottom lip. It wasn't enough; she needed more. She needed to feel his heat, to taste him, to feel wholly connected to him.

And, right at this moment, she wanted more than a kiss—she wanted it all. Cool sheets, naked bodies, him sliding into her and making her whole...

In his arms, she felt pretty and perfect—sensational, as if her sole purpose in life was to stand in the African sun and kiss him. If only he'd do it properly. Ella opened her mouth to demand more but, before she could utter a word, he captured her open mouth and slid his tongue inside. And she was suddenly on a bullet train travelling through a kaleidoscope of light and warmth, sensation and emotion. On one level she took in the details—his soft hair, his clever tongue, his big hand cupping her butt, the length and thickness of his erection. On another level, she was pure sensation—heat and colour and warmth and emotion...

This guy, she thought, her mind spinning, could *kiss*. If he was half as good, a quarter as good, in bed, she'd never recover. Wow, was she thinking of going to bed with him? Yes…yes, she was. Why wouldn't she? She'd had a few miserable months; didn't she deserve a little fun?

Ella heard Micah's low groan as her hands travelled up and down his back, and his kiss deepened when she pulled his shirt out of the back of his shorts so that she could feel his warm skin under her palms. So strong, so masculine… She wanted to kiss him here, at the base of his spine; and here, on the deep valley above his hard butt. There were other places she wanted to kiss, intimate spots she'd never explored before…

Micah placed his big hands on her cheeks and his kiss turned gentle, softer, a gradual dialling down of his passion. He pulled his mouth off hers and kissed her cheek, her nose and each of her closed eyelids before resting his forehead on hers. Like her, he was breathing heavily.

'Wow,' he whispered.

'That bad?' Ella asked, even though she knew it was anything but. But a little reassurance never hurt a girl.

'That good,' Micah said, wrapping his arms around her and pulling her into a tight hug. 'Hold on to me for a sec. I just need a moment to recover.'

She knew he didn't, not really, but she was happy to stand in his arms, her cheek on his chest, looking out at the valley overlooked by those impressive cliffs and hangouts. Somewhere in the distance, she could hear the chatter of a stream and the melodious tones of two women talking in Sesotho. She could stand like this for the rest of the afternoon. Being held by Micah was better than she'd ever imagined.

But in a minute he'd break the spell, suggest that they go to their hotel and finish what they started. Because a kiss like that was just the start of a pleasure-soaked journey, one that needed completion. It was, obviously, the natural outcome…

He was her boss, but in a six-steps-removed type of way, so the boss-employee dynamic wasn't, to her, much of a factor. And sleeping with Micah would be the perfect way to get her back in the dating game, to put the ghosts that hovered around her because of Pillay's behaviour to bed. She wasn't the type of girl who could easily separate sex from love. She thought the act was better when emotion was involved, but maybe sleeping with Micah would be a good way to get her sexual mojo back. If she'd ever had any.

In a couple of weeks, she'd be out of his life, so there was no way she'd allow herself to fall for him. Being with Micah would be a way to replace those bad sexual memories of Pillay's hot breath and clammy hands with some good ones. If she started feeling confident and attractive—who wouldn't feel like that after being with Micah?—maybe that would translate into her feeling confident about her life, would make her feel more self-assured. Sleeping with Micah would give her a new lease on life and would be a great way to kick-start her new life.

She had no fears of sleeping with Micah. Nothing about being with him, being held by him as tightly as she was made her have any flashbacks. She didn't feel constricted, scared or flustered, she just wanted more. So, yes, she was interested in sleeping with him, of course she was. She'd initiated that kiss and she'd all but climbed inside him while they'd been kissing. To men like Micah, kissing was the first stop on the destination, but…

But maybe it was wise to slow down…just a little. To stop, think and work out whether she was heading in the right direction. Being around Micah was like stepping into a Category Five tornado, and she felt caught up in its turbulence. She'd prefer to make the decision to sleep with him when she was feeling a little less storm battered and more like the self-confident person she so wanted to be.

Ella waited for his suggestion that they go, that they pick this up at their hotel, but instead of going there Micah patted the top of her bottom and pulled back from her. 'I'm starving. Why don't we head into Clarens and find a place to eat? I need to check my emails and return some calls before we head a few miles out of town for our next appointment.'

Right, that wasn't what she expected to hear. So what else could she do but nod her head and follow him to his car? And why did she feel so intensely disappointed?

CHAPTER FIVE

MICAH, AFTER CONSULTING the hotel receptionist, took Ella to the most popular restaurant in town for dinner. He couldn't remember when he'd last been in anything but a modern restaurant, an upscale jazz joint or as a VVIP in a happening club, but this place was a pleasant surprise.

The owners of this high-class eatery seemed obsessed with quality, from the astounding art on the walls, to the extensive range of excellent spirits behind the bar and the daily menu. This included chic dishes such as roasted quail with grapes, fennel-roasted pork belly and whipped-honey and lemon ricotta. If he were in the market for a gastro pub—and he might be in the future— this place would be of interest. It also happened to be within the grounds of their hotel, so it was an easy walk from their chalets, and he didn't have to worry about drinking and driving.

The décor was a mix of styles—wood, concrete, slightly rusted iron sheets and boldly coloured walls. He approved of the linen table cloths and serviettes and the quality glassware. He narrowed his eyes at a games room attached to the back of the restaurant containing a fine, antique billiards table, a vintage pinball machine and—*ugh*—a dartboard. It was currently occupied by a group of youngsters. The owners were making a mistake by not filling the space with tables. The rest of the joint was a fantastic blend of luxury and laid back, but that games room hindered rather than helped.

Standing at the modern, brushed-concrete bar, his lips still scorched from their earlier kiss, Micah looked in the counter-to-ceiling mirror behind the bar and watched Ella, who sat at a small table at the back of the room. She'd changed from her feminine dress into a pair of tight jeans and a simple navy-and-white-striped top. Ballet pumps covered her feet and she'd twisted her hair up into a loose knot on the back of her head.

She looked amazing, and her clothes told him that his choice of a more casual place to eat was spot-on. If he'd chosen one of the elegant restaurants in town, she might have felt pressured to continue what they'd started earlier and that was something he was desperate to avoid.

She might be on her way out of Le Roux Events— and, as a businessman, he regretted losing her talents— but he was still her boss for now. And he was very aware that, when a boss and employee became sexually involved, life could quickly become complicated. No, if Ella wanted more, she'd have to make the first move. Hell, she'd have to make *all* the moves.

Micah leaned his elbows on the bar, accepting it would be a while before the bartender took his order, and found he was happy to have a moment to think.

He knew women and thought he understood them but he found Ella both mystifying and fascinating. She was a combination of confident and skittish, scared and brave. She kissed like a dream and she could be either hellishly straightforward or very cagey. She was a study in contrasts—light and shade, monochrome and intense colour.

Initially, she'd been worried about being alone with him, but after just one day, and a hellfire-hot kiss, she seemed to have got over that. She now seemed at ease around him, thank God.

Their employer-employee relationship and her recent history were factors in his hesitancy about taking her to bed. But there was a bigger reason for his caution: for the very first time since Brianna's accident, he felt something more than lust, more than a man's normal desire for sex, for a release, for a few hours of fun on a mattress. Ella intrigued him, confounded him and made him want to know more…

Sure, he wanted to explore her beautiful body, but he also wanted to take a walk around her maze-like mind. And he wanted her to like him too—a terrifying thought and one he'd never admit to.

She'd seen past his act and had sussed out that he was a great deal more impatient and less charming than he generally allowed people to see. She'd ignored his stylish exterior and the cash in his wallet and had caught glimpses of the man he really was: abrupt and easily irritated. Ella innately understood that, under his surface, he was more driven and less charismatic, and his occasional prickliness didn't bother her.

But what was the point of letting her duck her head to see below his surface? Not only was she his employee—albeit not for much longer—but she was also leaving the country soon. He could give her some bed-based fun and physical pleasure, but nothing more because...

a) She'd recently been accosted by a person in power...

b) She'd made him feel too much far too quickly, and that was as dangerous as hell.

Not that he was thinking of her in terms of falling in love—that wasn't possible, given that he'd been vaccinated against that emotional virus twenty years ago He would never marry and have kids. How could he when he'd taken that away from Brianna, when his actions had resulted in her existing in a space somewhere between life and death?

He'd offloaded onto her, and then had cut off contact with her, and he should've known that she would be worried about him, that his silence would've driven her crazy. He should've anticipated her jumping in her car and trying to find him...

It was his fault.

'Sir, what can I get you?'

Micah ordered a beer for himself and a glass of excellent red wine for Ella and told himself to be sensible. He should ignore their attraction and stop thinking about that kiss, about how much he'd love to make love to her. No good could come of it. He didn't, after all, deserve good.

Micah heard a wave of noise coming from a small

room adjacent to the main pub, and looked across the crowded room to see a group of young adults playing pool and throwing back their drinks. There were going to be a couple of very sore heads in the morning, he thought.

So young. So dumb.

Micah paid for the drinks and picked up a couple of menus, tucking them under his arm. He walked back to Ella, placed her glass in front of her and handed her a menu.

'I'm starving,' Ella told him, opening it. She made her choice and he summoned a waiter and placed their orders before leaning back in his chair. He closed his eyes and allowed the music, the general noise and the occasional shouts from the rowdy group in the games room to wash over him. Unfortunately, his day was far from done, he still had hours of work ahead of him tonight. Le Roux International work didn't come to a stop because he was out of the office. But being anywhere with Ella was a nice respite.

'Why are *you* looking for a venue for your sister?'

Ella's question made his eyes fly open and he stared at her, caught off-guard. Because he was the family trouble-shooter, the guy who sorted out the drama, the one who had amends to make.

'Because my sister asked for help,' Micah told her, his tone warning her not to ask any more questions.

She chose not to hear it. 'Thadie has a very talented wedding planner and she strikes me as being smart. Her fiancé also has connections of his own. It's not *your* wedding so, again, why you?'

Everything snaked back to The Incident two decades before. Brianna was at the centre of that whirlpool but its ripples had affected so many people. Thadie had lost her heroine, the person she'd considered to be her big sister, her beloved babysitter. Theo and Liyana had lost their best friends, and they missed the vibrant girl who'd spent an enormous amount of time in their house. And he'd put Jago through hell as he'd not only had to deal with Bri's diagnosis but also Micah's own abhorrent behaviour.

Of course, he couldn't tell Ella any of that…but, for the first time ever, he wanted to.

Because he didn't want to spend the rest of the evening in awkward silence, Micah decided to give her an explanation he hoped would satisfy her curiosity.

'Thadie does some charity work, and, through her social media observations on being a single mother, has become one of the country's biggest influencers. But her full-time job is being a mum—her boys are her priority and looking after them takes up a lot of her time. She doesn't employ a nanny and Jago and me, our butler, Jabu, and Thadie's best friend, Dodi, are her backup system. We are who she calls when she needs time away from the kids, which she seldom does.

'She wanted to come on this trip with me to look at venues, but it wasn't feasible, as she has two charity events she can't miss. And Gus, the older of the twins, has a surgery scheduled.'

Ella leaned forward, immediately concerned for the health of a child she didn't know. 'I hope it isn't anything serious?'

He shook his head. 'No, he's having his tonsils out. Apparently, it's a minor op when you are three.'

He caught Ella's shudder. 'It is, but it's hell when you're an adult. I had mine out five years ago and I thought I was going to die, it was so painful. I really missed my mum that week.'

He allowed his fingers to drift across her hand, over her wrist. 'I lost my mum when I was nine. Not fun.'

Their eyes connected and he saw the pain and confusion he'd experienced in those green-gold-brown depths. Here was someone who understood how the ground could drop away from under your feet without a moment's notice.

'No, not fun.' Ella waved her hands, as if to swipe her words away. 'So, what did you think about venue number two?'

He appreciated the change of subject; he didn't talk about his mum, his childhood or life in the Le Roux household with anyone other than his siblings and, as a family, they didn't tend to look back.

'Venue two was a little bigger than venue one, but not as upmarket.'

Ella tucked a strand of hair behind her ears. 'I still think the venue needs to be in Johannesburg. It just makes sense for it to be there.'

'Thadie's wedding planner, as you know, is the best in the business and has contacts a mile long. She's spent days looking for a suitable venue and there's nothing.'

Ella pursed her lips. 'I don't believe that. There's got to be something.'

'Well, if you have any ideas, let me know, but in the

meantime we're going to keep looking for an alternative venue. We'll head back to Johannesburg tomorrow.
Where else do you think we should look?'

'What about Parys?'

The arty riverside town situated on the Vaal River
might be a good option: it was a wealthy and stunning
place with superb scenery.

'Look into it.'

Ella nodded. 'I will but I still think that—'

'That Johannesburg is where the wedding should
be.' Yeah, he got it, but there was nothing, and he
couldn't magic a venue out of thin air. What could he
do? Not keep looking and hope like hell something
turned up? No, he couldn't take that chance. He would
fix this for Thadie. Fixing stuff was what he did. Who
he was...

Another loud shout from the billiard room caught
their attention and everyone in the bar looked over to
where the kids were doing shooters. South Africa's
legal drinking age was eighteen but at times like this
Micah thought it should be raised to thirty or thirty-
five.

Their food arrived and Micah was happy to see Ella
tucking in with gusto. Unlike many women he knew,
she didn't push her food around the plate, pretend-
ing to eat but not making a dent in her meal. No, Ella
dove in and murmured her appreciation, closing her
eyes in pleasure as she chewed. She was such a sen-
sual woman but Micah knew she had no idea of her
impact. She glided when she walked, her face lit up
when she smiled and the corners of her eyes crinkled

just a little when she laughed. She turned heads, both male and female. She had presence, an energy, that couldn't be ignored.

By the time they finished eating, the party in the billiards room had turned loud and obnoxious. Ella finished her second glass of wine and scratched the side of her head. She nodded to the young adults. 'They are so inconsiderate; they're spoiling the place for everyone else.'

Well, yeah, kids did that. They didn't think of other people and never when alcohol was involved. He couldn't judge them too harshly; he'd done far worse than party it up in a bar.

'Ten more minutes and they'll be out of here,' he told Ella. The leader of the group was looking restless and Micah knew that he was bored. And where he went the others would follow. He was the guy others listened to, the party animal, the leader of the crew.

'What sort of teenager were you?' he asked Ella, interested in the answer. He was interested in everything about her. Smart and studious, he bet. Responsible and thoughtful.

She confirmed his thoughts when she answered. 'I was driven, I guess. I wanted to get my studies over with as quickly as possible so I could go out and work, earn some money.' He suspected that part of her need had been to get out of her house; she'd mentioned it had been chaotic. Before he could ask her a follow-up question, she asked a question of her own. 'And you? What kind of teenager were you?'

He debated whether to answer her but then shrugged.

What harm could it do? It wasn't as if he was going to tell her anything of consequence. At least, he hoped he wouldn't.

He picked up his nearly empty beer bottle and pointed it at the leader of the group. 'Do you see Mr Cool, the one with the ripped jeans, the *AC/DC* T-shirt and the designer trainers that retail at nearly three hundred pounds?'

The kid had his arm slung around a girl who wasn't as drunk as the others and looked as if she'd had enough. He'd seen that look on Bri's face often enough.

'I bet he has a very expensive car outside, something like a Range Rover, or an Audi TT, or a limited-edition Golf GTI. Something pricey and fast and red-hot. He clicks his fingers and girls come running and, if they don't, he shrugs off the rejection, calls them a waste of his time and moves on to the next in the line. If they do jump to do his bidding, he dumps them when he gets bored with them and, trust me, he has a very low threshold for boredom. He doesn't get told "no" often, or ever. He's out of control, and he knows it, but his pride won't let him admit it.'

Ella turned back to look at him, her expression puzzled. 'How do you know all that?'

'Because I was him,' Micah admitted. He shrugged and tried to smile. 'You asked me what I was like when I was young. I was like that.'

Ella started to protest but she'd barely started her sentence when Micah saw the older of the two bartenders cross the room towards the youngsters, a nervous look on her face. Micah pulled a face and mentally told her to look tough or else the kids would eat her up and spit her out. The kids noticed her approach and their expressions turned belligerent. This wasn't going to end well.

Micah looked around the room and silently cursed when he saw that everyone else was either eating or ignoring the situation. Mr Cool folded his arms and his male friends lined up behind him, a wall of arrogance and aggression. She was one person, not a knife-wielding group of thugs.

It was like sending in a poodle to deal with a pack of pit bulls. He stood and pushed up from the table. Time to get scary...

'Give me five minutes,' he told Ella. Slowly, hands in the pockets of his shorts, he meandered past the tables to the games area, coming to stand a few feet behind the bartender, who had no idea of his presence.

'I think it's time for you lot to go home,' the bartender said, her voice quavering.

'And how do you think you going to make us...?' Mr Cool's voice trailed off when he saw Micah and, yep, he paled just a bit. He was a big guy, far bigger than anyone in the room, and it was clear he knew that when he looked angry he could intimidate Satan himself.

'We'll quieten down,' he stated, his eyes darting to Micah and back to the bartender.

Micah shook his head and the kid winced. Mr Cool looked around at his mates, pushed back his chest and lifted his lip in a sneer. 'We might as well go, guys, this place is awful anyway. Never been so bored in my life.'

He pulled a set of keys from the back pocket of his

too-tight jeans and tossed them up in the air. He fumbled his first catch, just made the second and Micah knew he wasn't in a fit state to drive. None of them were.

Micah had been as full of arrogance and self-importance and had made a stupid, impulsive decision which had had far-reaching consequences. Life-changing, heart-breaking consequences. He still lived with the guilt and would for the rest of his life. If he could save another teenager from tragedy, he would, and he didn't care if he had to some knock some heads together to do it. Not that this situation would come to that. None of these kids could meet his direct gaze so he knew nobody would throw a punch. If they did, well, they'd test his Krav Maga skills, honed over years of training.

After asking, he ascertained they were staying within walking distance of the pub and could easily walk home.

'I'm not leaving my Rover here!' Cool told him hotly. 'Not a chance.'

Micah saw an empty wooden bowl on a shelf, grabbed it and held it out. 'Car keys, *now*.'

One by one, sets of car keys dropped into the bowl and Micah engaged in a staring contest with Cool until he dropped his keys inside the bowl too. He glared at the bartender. 'My car had better be safe when I come back for it or else!'

Micah ignored him and handed the bowl to the bartender. He brushed off her thanks and waited for the kids to leave before returning to Ella and rolling his eyes.

'That was pretty hot, Le Roux,' she said, her eyes holding admiration and more than a little lust. 'I like how you got them to listen with just a scowl and one raised eyebrow.'

He smiled. 'It's one of Jabu's favourite tricks. He never screamed or yelled, he just glared at me and lifted one eyebrow and I did whatever he asked, as quickly as I could.'

'Who is Jabu?'

'Butler, friend, the only father I ever really had,' Micah said, wondering why words flew from his mouth when he was around her. He drained his beer and pushed his chair back so that it rested on its back legs, giving him a better view of the exit and the kids heading towards the road.

'Why did you interfere?' Ella asked him. 'Most people wouldn't, they'd let the staff deal with them.'

Micah gestured to the bartender. 'She's their age, and timid. Do you really think they were going to listen to her?'

Ella shook her head. 'That's not why I'm asking. Why did *you* get involved?'

He knew she wasn't going to drop the subject. The vision of Brianna popped into his head, lying in that hospital bed, and he tasted the acrid hospital disinfectant at the back of his throat. He remembered her still body and her eyes, so blue and so vacant, staring at nothing.

Ella's hand gripped his and she squeezed his fingers. The hiss of pain jerked him back to the present.

'Come back from wherever you are, Micah. It's not a good place for you to be,' Ella told him in a fierce voice.

It was where he should be, Micah thought. He deserved, like Brianna, to be in no man's land. He looked down and away, cursing fate that Bri wasn't living her life out in the world, laughing and loving. She could be married by now, with a family. But she was stuck in that weird half-life and, to an extent, so was he.

He worked, looked after his family and worked some more. He exercised. He didn't have a personal life. He wasn't worthy of having one... What the hell was he doing here, spending time with Ella, chatting to her over dinner and a drink, as if this had the potential to go somewhere?

Sex was necessary, a great way to relieve stress, and he treated the woman he slept with well, but he never emotionally engaged with them. He didn't kiss them on balconies, tell them anything about his past and hold them tight, enjoying their softness and their femininity, feeling for the first time in years at peace in someone's arms.

He pushed back his chair with such force that it skidded across the floor. He pulled cash out of his wallet, tossed the notes onto the table and, without a word, walked away. He caught the confusion on Ella's face and knew he was behaving badly, but he needed air, he needed quiet and he needed to get away from her...

She saw too much, and worse—much worse—made him feel far too much. She was dangerous and he needed to remember that.

CHAPTER SIX

ELLA LOOKED DOWN at the money on the table and stared at Micah's retreating back, noticing the tension in his neck and shoulders. He looked as if he was carrying the world on his shoulders.

What on earth had she said? What had triggered his switch from being a charming dinner companion to a man who looked like she'd kicked him in the solar plexus and then stamped on his heart?

Ella caught the eye of the waitress, pointed at the cash on the table— far more than what their meals cost—and pushed back her chair. Walking slowly, she stepped into the still hot, fragrant summer night and looked up at the sky. Because this was mostly a rural area, the stars hung low in the sky, like sparkly little apples ready to be plucked off an intergalactic tree with wide branches.

The moon was a sliver in the sky and she remembered her mum describing it as 'God's thumbnail'. It was at times like these—times of change and uncertainty—that she missed her mum the most. She'd do anything to be able to call her up and ask for advice or to simply step into her arms for a long 'I've got you' hug.

Her mum had given the best hugs and, until this morning, she hadn't had a decent hug since she'd been sixteen years old. Her previous lovers hadn't been the 'cuddle her close' types.

Ella ignored the burn of tears in her eyes and rapidly blinked them away. Her dad didn't engage with her. Why did she keep thinking about him? Why couldn't she forget him—he obviously wanted her to—and move on with her life?

Because he was her dad, the only person she could call her own… Ella walked past the reception to the hotel and stepped onto the path that would take her to the attractive building that housed Micah's and her adjoining rooms. Their rooms shared a veranda and looked onto the rolling lawn that ended at a pretty pond. In the pale light on the veranda, she saw Micah leaning against the door to his room, arms folded and head bowed.

The world thought he was this charming, carefree character; sexy, successful and sophisticated. Oh, he was all those things, but also so much more. Underneath the sharp clothes and the designer stubble, the fancy watch and the smart car, was a man of unexplored depths, someone who had demons running after him with pitchforks.

Ella stopped on the path a little way from him, wondering what to say or how to act. Should she pretend that nothing had happened inside the bar, ignore his flash of deep unhappiness, his burst of temper? After what happened with Pillay, she thought she'd be scared to be alone with any man, but she was convinced Micah would rather cut out his kidney than hurt her or any other woman, child or animal.

No, whatever had happened had nothing to do with her. His anger had been self-directed, and she knew he was doing some intense self-flagellation. Words wouldn't help, Ella decided. Nothing she could say could bring him back from that dark place he was currently visiting. She could stand beside him and wait for him to return to her on his own, but who knew how long that would take? Or she could try and reach him another way...

Ella walked up the shallow steps to the veranda, stepped in front of him and gently pulled his arms apart so that she could wrap her arms around his waist and place her cheek on his thumping heart. He needed comfort, so she plastered her body to his, wanting to give him her heat and something to hang on to as he surfed those cold, dark winds.

He didn't touch her. His arms hung at his sides but after a minute, maybe more, she felt some of the tension leave his body and heard his deep sigh. She knew that he was coming back to her when he placed his big hands on her hips and when he turned his head to rest his lips in her hair. Knowing he needed more, that she needed more, she pulled back and placed her mouth on his, encouraging him to step out of the darkness and back into the light.

He tensed again so she probed the seam of his mouth with her tongue and, when he opened his mouth, she kissed him gently, silently telling him to concentrate on her, on how she made him feel.

Ella felt a long shudder run through him then his hand slid across her lower back and he pulled her into him. She felt his hard erection, the proof she needed that he was back with her, in the moment. He took control of their kiss and, with one swipe of his tongue, he pulled her into an alternative world, one where only he existed.

She didn't care that he was her boss, temporarily or otherwise, and that this might be awkward in the morning. All she knew for sure was that she wanted him.

And that maybe, just for tonight, he wanted and *needed* her. That was enough. That *had* to be enough.

Ella wrenched her mouth from his, pulled back and shoved her hand into the pocket of her jeans to pull out her electronic room key. She stepped around Micah, jammed her key into the slot and cursed when the room remained locked. She repeated the action, the door opened and she reached back to grab a handful of Micah's shirt to pull him into the room. As soon as he was inside, she wound her arms around his neck, found his mouth again and tried to tell him, in the only way she knew how, how much she wanted to see him naked, to know what it felt like to have his body on hers, in hers.

Micah groaned, pulled her closer and kissed her thoroughly, intensely, his hand in her hair to keep her mouth plastered to his.

She needed him in a way that felt both foreign and wonderful, scary and delightful. She was riding the world's most dangerous roller coaster, stowing away on a rocket ship, diving to dangerous depths without a mask...

And she was loving every second of it.

Micah gripped a handful of her hair, gently pulled her head back and, despite the darkness, she saw the look of intensity on his face, the heat in his eyes. 'Are we doing this, Ella? Having sex?'

Given her recent history, she understood that he wanted—*needed*—her verbal consent and she was happy to give it. It might be a mistake, but she'd face those consequences tomorrow. 'Yes, if you'd like to.'

His answer to that statement was to take her hand and place it on his erection. She sighed at how hard he was, how big. 'I'd like.'

Through the material of his trousers, Ella swiped her thumb across his shaft. She didn't drop her eyes from his and saw the flash of pleasure, heard his sudden intake of breath. He liked that, so she did it again.

Releasing a small growl, Micah bent his knees, wound his arm under her butt and lifted her. It felt natural for her to wind her legs around his waist, relishing his strength and power. She felt small next to him, completely feminine. His mouth closed around her nipple and he tongued her through the fabric of her top and bra. Annoyed by the barrier, she leaned back, trusting him not to drop her, and lifted her shirt up her chest and over her head. She kept her eyes on his face as she reached behind her and undid the snap of her bra, pulling it off to toss it to the floor. She saw his gaze lower to her chest to take in her pale skin, her breasts—smaller than she'd like—and puckered nipples.

His hand cupped a breast, lifted it up and his lips closed over her nipple, setting off another round of fireworks in her brain, down her spine, between her legs…

'Micah,' she moaned, spearing her fingers into his hair.

He lifted his head to look in her eyes, and she fell into all that blue. 'You are so beautiful.'

She wasn't but he made her feel that way. He was so big, completely and overwhelmingly masculine. But, as strong as he was, there was a part of him that could be bruised, that was tender, able to be hurt…

In Ella's eyes, that didn't make him less of a man, but more.

Micah carried her over to the bed in the centre of the room and gently lowered her down, stroking his big hands over her breasts before shedding his shirt and unsnapping the buttons of his jeans. His tattoo was a Māori-inspired design covering his right pec, and fabulously hot. He pushed his jeans down his hips, along with his underwear, and she saw his slim hips, those sexy hip muscles she'd imagined him having, the ridges of his cut stomach. Her eyes dropped down further but, before she could take in his length and thickness, he bent down to kiss her chest and her stomach. His hand played with the snap of her jeans. 'Let's get these off, shall we?'

He was checking in with her again, wanting to know if she was still on board, and Ella nodded. Micah removed her jeans and stared down at her lacy panties, a hand drifting over her hip and across her bare bottom. 'I love thongs,' he said, sounding hoarse.

She did too, but right now she wanted it off. Instead of removing the scrap of fabric, Micah stroked his finger over her, pushing the fabric down into her feminine lips where it soaked up her heat. Lying back on the bed, Ella placed her forearm over her eyes and, half-lifting up, tried to push Micah's hand to where she most wanted it—touching her in that special place.

He released a satisfied laugh before pulling the edge of her panties to the side and sliding his finger up and down, flirting with her core. Ella lifted her hips off the bed to increase the contact, needing more. Needing everything he could give her.

Micah lay down beside her, holding her face so that she looked at him. 'I want to go slow, but I need you, El.'

Ella found his erection and wrapped her hand around his girth, surprised when he hardened even more. 'I need you too. Now.'

'Condom,' Micah said, sounding desperate.

She didn't have any but, God, she hoped he did. Micah rolled off the bed, grabbed his jeans and yanked his wallet out of the pocket. Bank cards, cash and credit card slips fell to the floor. He swore creatively and then she heard his relieved sigh. He dropped his wallet and, still standing up, completely unselfconscious, ripped open the condom and rolled it down his shaft, a normally prosaic action made erotic by a sexy man.

Micah placed his knee on the bed and dropped his head to place his mouth on her, licking her once in a slow, hot slide. Ella gasped then released a heated groan and Micah slid into her, stretching her and filling every inch of her. He placed his hands on either side of her head and stared down at her as he pulled back and re-entered her, slowly, stunningly.

Ella licked her lips, needing his mouth. 'Kiss me, Micah.'

Micah dropped down and she caught a flash of intense blue before his tongue entered her mouth, echoing the movements of what was happening down below.

Ella felt as though she was both inside her body and out of it, a part of Micah but not, playing on the stars as well as riding the biggest of the ocean's waves. She was sex and sensation, on the bed and not; herself, but Micah too.

Sensation steadily built and she felt tears in her eyes, her heart filling with an emotion she couldn't identify. She'd had sex before but nothing like this, nothing so crazy wonderful, so startlingly sensational.

She felt herself standing on the edge of a cliff but not scared to walk off it, knowing she'd be caught and tossed up into the heavens, into that starry sky she'd admired earlier.

Ella dug her fingernails into Micah's butt and arched her hips, silently encouraging him to go faster, to take her higher. He responded immediately and pumped his hips, driving deeper into her, commanding her to feel all of him, to take every bit of pleasure she could.

His voice faded away, a wave of pleasure shoved her into the void and she tumbled and fell, rolled over and ignited in a fireball that was all heat and no pain, filled with colours she'd never experienced before.

She exploded and, a long time later, she floated

down, idly gathering her shattered pieces, slowly putting them back together.

When she was done, she realised Micah's face was on her neck, his arms cradling her head and his weight pushing her body into the mattress. It didn't matter that she couldn't breathe; he felt amazing.

As though reading her mind, Micah rolled off her onto his back, his hand patting the space between them to come to land on her thigh. Ella turned her head to see that his eyes were still closed and that he was breathing rapidly, his chest pumping up and down. A fine layer of perspiration covered his neck, shoulders and chest.

He looked like a Greek god who'd just run a marathon. So sexy...

Micah rolled his head to the side to look at her. 'Wow.'

He'd said the same thing when he'd kissed her earlier. 'That bad?' she asked, knowing it wasn't.

He squeezed her thigh and sent her a long, slow, skin-melting smile. 'I don't know. I might have to do that again so that I know it wasn't an aberration.'

Ella smiled, happy to see that his ghosts were gone. 'I'm happy to help you come to a definite answer.'

He grinned and kissed her briefly before rolling off the bed. He walked into the bathroom and, when he returned, he bent down to pick up his jeans and swiftly pulled them on. Ella sat up abruptly. 'Are you leaving?' she demanded, confused.

Micah kissed her nose. 'We need more condoms, sweetheart. Do you have any?'

Condoms? No! She hadn't thought she'd be having sex any time soon, so it wasn't something she'd stocked up on. 'Uh…no.'

'Didn't think so. I'll be right back.' Micah straightened and pointed a finger at her. 'Your only job is to remove those panties.'

It was only then that Ella remembered that she had them on.

Ella woke up and wasn't surprised to find herself alone in her big double bed. She rolled over and peered off the end of the bed but, as she expected, Micah's clothes were gone too.

Ella stretched, arched her back and pointed her toes before slumping back into the mattress. The bedside clock said it was twenty past six and, through the gap in her closed curtains—though she didn't remember pulling them closed last night—she saw that it was raining steadily. What she most wanted to do was to roll over and go back to sleep but, having failed to find a suitable venue in Clarens—they'd heard that venue three was even smaller than the others—they were heading back to Johannesburg this morning. She assumed she would be driving, and she'd need a vat of coffee and a few energy drinks if that was the case.

Still naked, Ella sat up and wrapped her arms around her bent knees, staring at the water colour of the mountains on the wall across the room. She'd made love to Micah Le Roux last night and it had been…

Well, fabulous. Divine, wonderful, amazing.

They'd made love twice, and done some hot exploring in the shower afterwards, and she'd loved every minute with him. He hadn't banished the memories of Pillay's hot breath and sweaty hands, of him pinning her against the wall and trying to force his hand between her legs, but they weren't as oppressive any more. They'd somewhat faded.

From now on, when she thought of being intimate with a man, she'd remember Micah's sexy mouth and broad hands sliding across her skin, the way he'd turned her blood to hot syrup and how he'd raised fireworks on her skin. She wasn't one to rush into relationships—she was terrified of rejection and broken expectations—but she'd no longer be driven by fear. She was, thanks to Micah, in a different place now.

But Ella also suspected that any man she dated in the future, every future lover, would always be compared to Micah. She genuinely didn't believe last night could be improved on. It was the perfect first night with a new lover, both hot and sweet, tender and tempestuous.

But Micah didn't want a relationship and neither did she. It was a one-night stand, something that wouldn't be repeated. She now knew she could date again, maybe even sleep with a man again, and that was a relief.

But Ella still doubted she could have a relationship again. Because some scars didn't heal as quickly as others. Her father had mentally and emotionally disappeared on her after her mum had died. He had, in a sense, chosen to emotionally abandon her. Yes, he'd provided for her, and paid her school and university fees, but as she'd got older the gap between them had widened.

She'd always thought that, at some point, they'd find their way back to each other, but after years of trying she now knew they never would because it took two to reconnect. Being disappointed by your dad was a special type of hell and one that caused deep scars that would take a lifetime to heal. If they ever did.

And, if she couldn't trust her father—the one man who was supposed to love her, listen to her, to be there for her, to believe in her, to support and protect her— how could she trust any other man? Her father had taken away her trust in men, Pillay her trust in herself.

But maybe, thanks to Micah, she was regaining some of her self-confidence. There was something incredibly empowering about having a good, sexy-as-sin man interested in her. He wasn't the charming, charismatic man the world thought he was... No, that wasn't right, of course he was charming and very charismatic. But he wasn't *only* that man. He was deeper and more complicated than people suspected.

Micah had, she was sure, lived a thousand lives and not all of them were good. Things had happened to him that had caused deep, wide wounds, injuries that still made him ache and seethe. He was both hurt and angry, wounded and wishful.

But she couldn't get involved, couldn't let him get to her. She already cared far too much about what Micah thought about her. If she spent more time with him— assuming that he wanted a repeat of last night—she'd be in trouble, the 'losing her heart' kind of trouble.

Even if she hadn't been planning to emigrate, there'd have been no hope of a relationship developing between Micah Le Roux and her. He didn't do relationships. According to social media and the press, he'd never had a girlfriend who'd lasted more than a few months, and she couldn't risk having someone she cared for disappoint her again. She was a normal working girl; he was a fast-moving billionaire businessman. Their lives had temporarily intersected but life would, as it inevitably did, pull them apart.

She had to be sensible, smart and protect her heart. She was the only one who could do that. Because, if she didn't look after herself, no one else would.

Knowing his concentration was shot, and that he wouldn't get much work done if he tried, Micah elected to drive them back to Johannesburg. Never before had a woman managed to pull his focus off work but Ella was one of a kind.

She was a series of firsts, he decided as he pulled over to pass a fuel tanker. The first employee he'd got naked with, the first woman he'd spent most of the night with—he'd only left her room when the red numbers on her bedside clock had flipped to six a.m.—and the first he'd wanted to keep in bed for the rest of the day.

The Bentayga's fancy computer flipped the windscreen wipers onto fast and Micah raised his eyebrows as the sound of thunder drowned out his favourite radio station. Rain fell in heavy sheets and, because the visibility was terrible, he slowed down. At this rate, it was going to take them for ever to get home.

He glanced to his left and saw that Ella was busy on her phone, looking at pictures of a grey-blue building. Judging by her cool but friendly attitude this morning, no one would've guessed they'd spent the night together or that he'd, in turn, made her scream and sigh. When she'd appeared in the dining room for breakfast, she'd acted as if nothing had happened and he was both grateful and irritated. Grateful because he didn't want her to start acting like his girlfriend, and irritated because she was behaving as if she hadn't rocked his world.

Micah ran a hand over his face, knowing that he sounded like an insecure kid. They'd had sex, great sex, and if she wasn't going to make a big deal of it, neither was he. He was older, and better, than that.

'What are you doing?' he asked, needing for some stupid reason to hear the sound of her melodious voice.

She looked up quickly before looking back down at her phone. 'I'm still trying to find a Johannesburg-based option for your sister's wedding.' She obviously caught something on his face because her lips twisted. 'I know you think it's a fool's errand, but I'm convinced there's something out there that would be a brilliant venue.'

'I can't stop you from looking but I don't think you're going to find anything. Thadie's wedding planner is—'

'The best in the business and she has incredible contacts…blah, blah, blah,' Ella muttered, eyes on her phone. 'I'm still wrapping my head around her losing the booking at The Gables.'

'I don't think it's fair to blame her,' Micah said.

'Oh, I blame everyone involved,' Ella quickly responded. 'The whole thing was badly handled.'

Really? 'Why do you think that?'

'Firstly, if I were the owner of the hotel, or the hotel's function manager, on receipt of those emails I would've got on the phone, or even driven to the wedding planner's offices, and demanded a face-to-face meeting to find out what went wrong. I can't understand why they didn't, because they've blotted their name with every wedding and event planner in the city now.'

'So you think the hotel messed up?'

Ella pushed her straight hair back over her shoulders. She wore another dress today, this one fitted to the waist and flaring over her hips in a navy-and-white polka-dot print.

'Of course they did. Badly. If you can't trust your vendors to call you when a problem arises, how can you use them ever again? Trust me, The Gables are going to regret this. And I can't understand why Anna didn't scream and shout and dance on the hotel manager's desk until they reinstated the original booking. I think she let The Gables off the hook far too easily.'

Interesting. When he'd heard about the cancellation and the snafu, he'd gone into problem-solving mode and, after hearing that it would be impossible to hold the wedding there, hadn't given The Gables another thought. His entire focus had been on finding a new venue, sorting out the problem and keeping everyone happy.

And maybe Anna de Palmer-Whyte wasn't as hot as everyone thought.

Micah saw a herd of cattle at the side of the road and, knowing how unpredictable they could be, slowed down a little more. 'What's your favourite type of event to organise?' he asked, interested in everything about her.

Ella half-turned to face him and smiled. 'Weddings, of course. But, as I said yesterday, I'd like to specialise in family events, like Anna does. That's the dream, but specialising takes connections at the highest level, connections I don't have. Maybe when I get to the UK I can look at doing smaller, more intimate events. I'm good at those.'

He believed her. 'Why are you emigrating?'

Ella removed her water bottle from the cup holder and tipped it up to her mouth. Micah remembered those lips under his, sliding across his chest, down his stomach. Lower...

He squirmed in his seat but Ella seemed oblivious to his discomfort. 'There's nothing and no one left for me in South Africa.'

That was a hell of a statement. 'At all?'

Ella replaced her water bottle and tucked her leg behind her knee, her torso angled towards him.

'I'm an only child of only children. My dad still lives in Durban but we don't talk.'

'Why not?' he asked.

'After my mum died, our relationship significantly deteriorated.' It was an answer but not an explanation.

'We're not on speaking terms any more. His choice,' Ella added.

Micah knew that something major had happened for all communication to end. He'd lived a scenario exactly like that. And he knew how painful it was to see your family ripped apart. He at least had Jago and Jabu and, although she'd been so young at the time, Thadie. Ella, it seemed, had nobody. His heart ached for her.

Ella turned the silver ring on her right middle finger round and round. 'I just want a new start, another one. He—' She abruptly stopped talking and turned to sit in her seat properly, staring out of the side window.

'Will you tell me what happened?' he asked quietly. 'Between you and your dad?'

'I don't want to rehash it, Micah.'

She shrugged and bent down to fiddle in her bag. When she sat up again, she slid sunglasses onto her face, despite it being a grey and wet day without a hint of a glare. She didn't want him to see her eyes, to catch a glimpse of her thoughts.

Why did Ella hiding from him cause him such frustration? Why did he want to explore her mind as well as her body? He wanted to be the one person she could open up to, to feel safe with…physically and emotionally. Why her? And why now? What was it about Ella that made him forget why he was the way he was—an extroverted loner? There were few people he let into his inner world… Jago, Thadie and Jabu. Brianna, back in the day. People had to earn a place to eat at his table and he seldom gave anyone the chance to do that. But here he was, asking Ella to open up, and considering doing the same for her.

And it was funny how, since meeting Ella, he was thinking about Brianna more than he had in years. She would've liked Ella, and vice versa. He could see them being friends, laughing together over something he did or said. Missing Brianna came in waves and, right at this moment, he felt as if he was drowning. His eyes burned, his heart felt like a petrified piece of wood and he couldn't get enough air into his lungs.

Ella's hand on his leg, her fingers tightening on his thigh, pulled Micah out from under that cold wave.

'You've gone to that dark place again,' Ella stated quietly. 'As I said last night, it's not a good place for you to be.'

He sent her a look and, when she didn't ask a follow-up question, when she didn't push or pry, he sighed. 'You are the least curious, least pushy woman I have ever met.'

'I'm not sure if that's a compliment or a criticism. Do you want me to push and pry?'

Micah shuddered. 'God, no!'

Ella pushed a strand of hair behind her ear. 'It's raining hard, and the road is busy. I don't think it's a good time for deep and intense conversations, Micah.'

Right. Okay then. Maybe it was better if they didn't talk; he did need to concentrate. But after five minutes, curse him, he did start to miss the sound of her voice. He turned to look at her, thinking they could discuss something, anything, but found her curled up on the seat, fast asleep.

She remained like that until they hit the outskirts of Johannesburg.

CHAPTER SEVEN

ELLA PULLED UP next to a BMW convertible, top down, and lifted her bag off her passenger seat, hauling in a series of deep breaths to calm her racing heart. Micah had dropped her at her flat yesterday and kissed her goodbye without making arrangements for them to meet over the weekend. Ella had tried hard, really hard, not to feel disappointed. They'd only slept together, she reminded herself, they weren't in a relationship.

So she was surprised to get a text message that morning, demanding her presence at a meeting at Hadleigh House at ten. Ella had thought she'd spend her Saturday morning researching venues in Parys but here she was, ten minutes early, at one of the oldest and most historic estates in the city. Ella stepped out of the car, slammed the door and looked up at the magnificent, massive double-storey house with its shingled roof and ivy-covered walls.

Curious, she ignored the imposing front door, walked round the side of the house and sighed at the magnificent English-style country garden, the old and dignified oak trees and the dark-blue swimming pool.

It would make the most magnificent wedding venue, Ella decided. If Thadie pared down her guest list and decided to have a garden wedding, she could maybe accommodate two, three hundred people here, maybe more. Back in the day, this house had been the gathering place for the elite of Johannesburg mining society, and the house had played host to soirées, balls and tennis parties. She could see a huge, romantic tent on the deep-green swathe of lawn to her right, fairy lights in the trees, a gazebo holding a dance floor, roses floating on the surface of that huge pool…

But the idea of having a wedding here sparked a memory. She dimly recalled another house, old and lovely, somewhere in this area. It was another old Victorian, one of the grandest mansions in the city. She'd read about it when she'd first come to the city and for some reason—she knew not what—it floated into her brain when she thought about a garden wedding.

The Le Rouxs could make another fortune hiring out Hadleigh House. With its thick, lush lawn, extensive, colourful rose garden and magnificent trees, it was the perfect venue for an intimate wedding. But Thadie and Clyde didn't want intimate, they wanted a glitzy, glam, see-and-be-seen wedding. And there were few places that weren't soulless convention centres that could give them what they wanted—romance and soul, luxury and loveliness.

'Welcome to Hadleigh House.'

Ella smiled, turned around slowly and saw Micah standing on the cobbled path behind her. His hair was damp and pushed back from his face, which still hadn't seen a razor, and he was dressed in a navy linen shirt, white tailored shorts and expensive leather flip-flops. He looked as though he could star in one of those glamourous adverts for perfumes Ella couldn't afford, which always seemed to be set in the Ionian Seas.

She wanted him to take her to bed. Right now.

Ella gave herself a mental slap and pulled what she hoped was an impersonal smile onto her face. 'Nice place, Micah.'

He looked round and she caught the flash of affection in his eyes, pride on his face. 'It's home. I love it here.'

He didn't make a move to usher her into the house so Ella stayed where she was, happy to feel the sun on her bare shoulders. She wore a pale-blue and white sleeveless jumpsuit today and flat-soled sandals. She'd pulled her hair up into a messy knot on top of her head and wore minimal make-up. It was, after all, a Saturday.

Ella looked up and counted ten windows widely spaced on the second floor of the mansion. 'Big place,' she observed.

He nodded his agreement. 'I live here with my twin, Jago. We recently renovated the house and we have separate, private apartments in each wing, though we currently share the kitchen, downstairs entertainment areas, the deck, pool and, obviously, the garden. If either of us decide to bite the bullet and marry—'

'A fate worse than death,' Ella said, her tongue in her cheek.

He lifted his eyebrows. 'For me, it would be.'

It was a warning, Ella thought, a subtle way to remind her that, while they'd slept together, there was no possibility of more. The warning was unnecessary because trust was impossible. And a relationship without trust was a bird without wings.

Not waiting for her to comment on his answer, he continued. 'As I was saying, if we want more privacy, Hadleigh can provide enough space and distance to make it feel like two separate homes.'

Micah gestured for her to join him on the path and she followed him around the corner of the building to a vast, covered entertainment area featuring an outdoor kitchen, bar, gas barbecues, a dining table that could seat twenty and many plump couches and outdoor chairs.

Nice. Very nice indeed.

'Are you and your twin close?' Ella asked him, smiling at the two hammocks strung from the beams in the far corner of the veranda.

'Very,' Micah told her, placing a hand on her back as they hit the slate steps leading up to the veranda. Ella wished she could simply hang out in the space, maybe lie on one of those luxurious loungers beside the pool, take a dip, or sit in the ten-man hot tub.

'Jago won't be at this meeting. It'll just be Thadie and her bridesmaid Alta, Clyde's stepsister.'

She followed Micah across the veranda into another outdoor seating area, which could be closed off from the elements with bi-fold doors. This room sported black-and-white-striped couches, cherry-red armchairs, bold cushions and even bolder art on the walls. Ella, in sensory overload, was finding it difficult to concentrate. There was so much to look at and take in.

'Where's her fiancé? Her maid of honour? Actually, who is her maid of honour?'

'Dodi Lewis. She owns Love & Enchantment, the wedding dress salon. Dodi has a busy morning at work and I'm not sure what Clyde's excuse is.' Ella caught the bite of irritation in his voice and wondered if he approved of his sister's fiancé.

Then again, Thadie was a grown, independent woman and didn't need her brother's approval.

'We're meeting in the library.'

Ella followed him down a hallway, stopping briefly to take in the magnificent hall, with its Harlequin tiled floor and matching, hand-carved staircases, and caught a peek through a doorway of a sleek, glossy, gourmet kitchen with acres of granite countertops.

Exceptional art decorated the walls and massive bouquets of roses, hand-cut and probably from the garden, perfumed the air. Sculptures, bronzes and ceramics sat on antique tables and Ella kept her arms folded and her bag tucked by her side so that she didn't knock anything over. They'd have insurance but some of their objects looked irreplaceable. This was, by far, the grandest house she'd ever visited.

Micah stepped back to let her precede him into a double-storey library, shelves extending up so high that a ladder was attached to a railing twenty feet in the air enabling the reader to get a book from the top shelves. A big wooden desk dominated one half of the room and, at the other end, two fat, dark leather couches sat in front of a pair of French doors which opened into the garden.

She immediately recognised Thadie Le Roux, with her big eyes, flawless light-brown skin and her famous mother's incredible cheekbones. She turned at their entrance and her smile was Julia-Roberts-wide. God, she was gorgeous.

The woman next to her with gold hair, pasty skin and narrow eyes paled beside her. Thadie wore a bright-yellow sundress and sandals whereas the other woman wore a revealing top, a far too short black mini-skirt, and three-inch heels. Not to mention pursed lips and a scowl...

Thadie jumped to her feet and Ella took in her height. She was close to six feet and curvy. As she held out her hand in greeting, their eyes connected and, within those dark-brown depths, Ella saw warmth, a hint of panic and maybe a touch of *what the hell am I doing?*

Micah introduced her to his sister, and then to Alta, Clyde's stepsister, who didn't bother getting to her feet.

'Are the twins still with Jabu, Micah?' Thadie asked him as she sat down and crossed her long, slim legs.

'Yes, they are in the greenhouse. Mkulu's probably got them filling pots with compost or digging for worms in a flower bed.'

Alta gasped, horrified. 'But that's unsanitary!'

Thadie smiled. 'Little boys like dirt and digging in the soil, and being outside helps build up their immunity. Ella, please take a seat.'

Thadie gestured her to the couch and Ella sat down,

placing her tote bag at her feet. Micah offered her something to drink, and when she asked for coffee he nodded. A solid-silver tray sat on the coffee table and held a Chinese-looking teapot and thin-as-paper teacups on equally thin saucers.

'I'll just go make you a fresh cup,' Micah said.

'Just ring for the butler,' Alta told him.

Micah's lips tightened at being told what to do in his own house. 'As I said, Jabu is with the twins in the greenhouse and, even if he wasn't, I would never interrupt what he was doing to demand he bring me a cup when I could so easily get it myself. I'm rich, not spoiled,' Micah told her with an easy smile, his good humour restored.

Ella knew that Alta wanted to ask him what the point was of employing a butler if he didn't buttle. Was that even a word?

Thadie waved at a plate holding exquisite looking, one-bite cakes covered with a mirrored chocolate glaze. 'Please have one. They're divine, and I've already eaten three, so help me out here.'

Ella grinned, loving her honesty and, because she hadn't had breakfast and adored chocolate, took a tiny cake. 'Thanks.'

'You're not going to fit into your very expensive wedding dresses if you keep eating those,' Alta said, sounding snide.

Thadie just grinned. 'Of course I will! I run ten miles a day on the treadmill and another ten chasing the boys. And life is too short not to eat chocolate!'

Ella instinctively liked her. She just as instinctively

didn't like Alta, with her plummy accent and cool eyes. For Thadie's sake, she hoped Clyde was a lot warmer than his stepsister.

Thadie leaned forward and briefly rested her fingers on Ella's arm. 'Thank you so much for helping Micah to find a new venue.'

Ella was about to respond when Alta spoke. 'If your very experienced, unbelievably connected wedding planner can't find you a venue, Thadie, then I doubt Bella—'

'My name is Ella,' Ella mildly corrected her.

Alta didn't miss a beat. 'Will be able to find you a suitable venue. I strongly suggest you postpone the wedding and rebook the venue and vendors.'

Ella looked from Thadie to Alta and back again. Alta sat up straight and was as tightly wound as piano wire. Thadie, who'd kicked off her sandals and tucked her feet up under her bottom, looked relaxed and unfazed. This was, after all, her childhood home.

'I have complete faith in Micah,' Thadie told Alta, before flashing Ella her mega-watt smile. 'And you, of course, Ella.'

Ella thanked her but refrained from telling her that her faith might be misplaced. And optimistic. She wondered if she should try to temper Thadie's expectations but, before she could decide, Micah walked in, holding an enormous mug in his hands.

He handed it to Ella. 'Milk, no sugar. Strong.'

They'd often stopped for coffee on their trip to Clarens and back and Micah had surprised her by not having expected her always to do the coffee run. He'd asked her how she took her coffee and remembered. It was such a little thing and it shouldn't make her feel tingly. And special. Most of all, special. Micah, she told herself, was a super-smart guy and no doubt he remembered lots of little things, often.

Ella took the mug, wrapped her hands around it and took a grateful sip. Great coffee, she decided. Expensive coffee.

Yum.

Micah ignored Alta's gesture for him to sit next to her—ah, so that was the way that wind blew!—and sat down on the leather ottoman at a right-angle to Ella, their knees inches apart. He rested his forearms on his thighs. Ella looked at his broad hands with their long fingers, and was transported back to how those hands had stroked her from hip to breasts, how his fingers had slid between her legs...

'Don't you think so, Ella?' Micah's question was accompanied by a nudge to her knee, and she jerked her head up to look into those amused blue eyes. He was laughing at her, as if he knew exactly where her thoughts had wandered to. Dammit, she hated it when he seemed to read her mind.

'Sorry, I missed that,' she apologised, blushing.

'Micah was just saying that none of the venues in Clarens was suitable,' Thadie explained. 'I wanted to know whether you agreed.'

Ella crossed her legs, leaned forward and nodded. 'There are some lovely venues, but some aren't big enough, some aren't luxurious enough, some are just blah.'

'So what's the bottleneck?' Thadie asked, her intelligent gaze meeting Ella's. She narrowed her eyes the same way Micah did when he was focused on a problem—or making love to her—and tapped her index finger on her knee, the same way her brother did. They looked nothing alike, but both had similar mannerisms and a no-nonsense way of looking at a problem.

'The problem is that you don't have enough time, Thadie! If you postponed the wedding, you'd give everyone some breathing room!'

Thadie didn't acknowledge Alta's outburst, but Ella noticed her pinched face and the hard twist of her lips. Why was Alta one of Thadie's bridesmaids? They didn't seem to be friends, or in any way close. Was she just there because she was Clyde's stepsister?

'Ella?' Thadie asked, steel in her still sweet-smile.

Right, business. 'I think it's a combination of all three issues. You want a huge venue that is special and luxurious, able to accommodate many people. And you want it soon, when most venues have been booked for a year, sometimes two.'

'She's Thadie Le Roux,' Micah said. 'She's one of the most famous women in the country and that should count for something.'

He said it as a statement of fact, without a hint of elitism or boasting, and Ella couldn't take offence at that.

'Yes, I am. I am also marrying one of the most famous men in the country,' Thadie said, sitting up and dropping her feet. She sent Ella a rueful smile. 'But hotels are not going to bump a bride for me, especially at this late date. And they shouldn't. I'd hate for a bride to lose her big day because of me; that would be dreadful.'

'Not finding a decent venue would also be dreadful, a complete disaster. Really, you should postpone!'

Wow, Alta really wasn't bringing anything to this conversation. Ella decided to follow Thadie's lead and ignore her. 'Micah mentioned looking for a venue somewhere in the Drakensberg or the KwaZulu Natal Midlands...'

'But you don't think there's anything,' Thadie stated.

Ella wrinkled her nose. 'There are some big operations, and maybe something will turn up; it's worth a look.'

But how on earth was she going to be able to spend more time with Micah without being in his arms, in his bed? It was supposed to have been a one-night thing but, man, she wanted more. But Micah wasn't a 'more' type of guy and, even if he were, he'd never look at her in a 'let's have a relationship' way. She came with too much baggage. She had daddy and trust issues, disappointment issues, being believed issues. Finding her confidence issues.

A relationship was impossible.

Ella looked at Micah. 'If you like, I can go drive down myself, scout out the venues and report back. If there is anything viable, you could then come down.'

Thadie sent Micah a guilty look. 'I know how busy you are, Micah, and that you can't afford to take time away from the office. Ella seems sensible and straightforward, so I'd be more than happy to trust the search to her.'

Micah surprised her by shaking his head. 'No, I said I'd do this, and I'm doing it. I'll—*we'll*—find you a wedding venue, Thadie. I promise.'

Ella winced, wishing he hadn't said the P-word. She didn't know if she could fulfil that promise. But maybe this was a good time to raise another option. 'Would you be open to doing something different?'

Thadie shrugged. 'Like?'

'I'm thinking of a flower-filled atrium within a botanical garden. An old house or a mansion, a warehouse or an industrial building.'

Ella waited for the response to her out-of-the-box suggestions and, while Thadie and Micah thought about her suggestions, Alta erupted. 'My brother will never agree to exchange vows in a factory!'

Thadie ignored Alta again—something, Ella was convinced, she did quite often. 'Actually, Anna and I were just talking about that—exploring alternative ideas. We even thought about trimming the guest list so that we could be married here, at Hadleigh House— it's always been my dream to be married at home—but Clyde and my mum vetoed that idea. As they pointed out, it's too late to un-invite people to our wedding.'

But maybe, since both she and Anna were exploring other options, and if the wedding gods were on her side, Thadie would still have an incredible reception in a beautiful, unusual place.

'On Clyde's behalf, I absolutely insist on having the reception somewhere decent!' Alta spluttered.

Decent, to Alta, meant a five-star hotel, upmarket and luxurious. Thadie caught her eye and Ella suspected she wanted to do a massive eye-roll. As the bride, Ella thought she was being remarkably patient.

Thadie stood up, smoothed down her dress and slid her feet into her sandals. 'I need to get going.' She kissed Micah's cheek before turning to Ella and holding out her hands. Ella was surprised when Thadie squeezed her fingers and dropped a kiss on her left cheek, then her right. 'It was so lovely meeting you. Thank you for your help. I'm so appreciative. Maybe you, Anna and I could meet and we could throw some ideas around.'

Ella knew how possessive planners could be about their functions and internally winced. 'I don't think Anna would appreciate my input.'

'Anna is lovely, and not at all pretentious or protective of her turf. And, since this is becoming a wedding from hell, she'd welcome any input.'

Yeah, but not from someone so far down the events-planning ladder. But, God, being able to say that she'd worked with Anna de Palmer-Whyte, even for a day, would be a great, gold shiny star on her résumé.

But she wouldn't wait for Anna's call, that would just be setting herself up for disappointment.

Seeing that Alta was also preparing to leave, Ella concluded that the meeting was over and picked her tote bag up off the floor. Micah didn't suggest she hang around so she followed his sister into the hall. Thadie said goodbye to Alta and told them she was going out of the back door to fetch the boys from the greenhouse. Ella, Alta and Micah walked in silence to where Alta's and her cars were parked.

At her convertible, Alta kissed Micah's cheek, placed her hand on his chest and looked up into his face. 'It really will be so much better if Thadie postponed the wedding, Micah. So much easier, less *messy*.'

Ella looked away and swallowed her growl as Alta stroked Micah's chest as she would a fur stole. Hot and sticky jealously lodged in her throat.

'It's Thadie's wedding and she calls the shots, Alta,' Micah told her, not bothering to remove her hand from his chest. *Grr...*

'But you can persuade her, I'm sure,' Alta said, lowering her voice an octave. Then she stood up on her toes and dropped another too-long kiss on his cheek. 'Call me.'

Ella bit the inside of her own cheek as Micah opened Alta's car door and she deliberately flashed him most of her slim thigh as she settled into the seat. She gunned the engine, sent Micah another sultry smile and reversed, narrowly missing Ella's car.

What a...

'Wow. She's...prickly, isn't she?'

And she's got her eye on you...

'Alta? She's okay, she's just highly strung.'

Guys often used that as an excuse for a woman who was a complete witch. 'She doesn't like your sister much, does she? Why is she one of her bridesmaids?' Ella asked.

Micah looked genuinely surprised. 'What are you talking about?'

Oh, come on, it was *so* obvious. 'She does not like Thadie. At all.'

'You got that from one meeting?' Micah asked, and his amused and dismissive tone irritated her.

'Yes, I did.' Ella tipped her head back to look up at him. 'Be careful of her, she's not good for your sister.'

'She's harmless,' Micah scoffed. 'You're overreacting.'

You're crazy, you're overreacting, you're nuts. I don't believe you. I can't trust what you say.

She'd heard all the comments and every variation of the theme made her clench her jaw and grind her teeth.

How could he so easily have believed her about being sexually accosted but not believe her about this? His rejection of her opinion reminded her of how her dad refused to believe her when she'd said her mum was sick, of Winters brushing her off when she'd told him his best client had forced his attentions on her. She opened her mouth to argue her point, to stand up for herself, but the words stuck in her throat, creating an acidic slick.

Alta was Thadie's friend, and the wedding party had nothing to do with her, so she should just leave the subject alone and shrug off Micah's casual dismissal.

But it still made her stomach knot and her lungs burn. And, even if she'd had a right to an opinion on Thadie's and Alta's friendship, she knew that she didn't have the confidence and self-assurance to defend her judgement.

Before Pillay and her experience with the Human Resources people at Le Roux Events, she'd been able to stand up for herself, to defend her point of view. Ella knew that she wasn't the most confident person in the world but at least she'd been able to function. These days, she over-analysed everything and overreacted and, whenever she found herself at odds with someone about something—even something as small as Alta's and Thadie's relationship she felt like a balloon collapsing in on itself as it lost air.

She hated it, hated feeling less than, feeling small, rejected. Hated that even the smallest thing could affect her so much.

Needing to leave, Ella spun round, climbed into her car and pulled on her seatbelt, forcing it into its catch. She turned the key in the ignition but it didn't catch, so she banged her fist against the steering wheel and cranked it again.

'Ella, hold on! What's going on?' Micah demanded, bending his knees to look through the open window.

'Nothing,' Ella muttered. It was a weak response, a cop-out, but what else could she do? Blub on his shoulder, moan about how unfair life was, how she was still affected by Pillay's actions, how *less than* she felt? He'd find excuses and explanations and then pat her on the shoulder.

No, thank you.

Just once, just once in her life, she wanted to feel less isolated, to feel as if she had someone on her side, someone who always took her seriously and cherished her. But that wasn't going to happen, not any time soon. And Micah wasn't that person. Shaking her head, Ella turned the key again and this time the car fired up. Ignoring Micah, she slapped it into gear and turned to look behind her so she could start reversing.

'Come back inside, Ella.'

She heard the irritation in his voice, along with a healthy dose of *I don't know what just happened*.

Ella pushed the button to raise her window and ignored him calling her name. She reversed, shoved the car into gear to go forward and out of the corner of her eye saw Micah slap his hands on his hips, confused.

Talking wouldn't help. This was her issue, not his, and he was her lover, not her therapist. No, it was better to leave, to deal with her feelings in her way and on her own. After all, it was what she did best.

She was tempted to stop and explain but he wouldn't understand. Nobody did. So she drove on.

CHAPTER EIGHT

Micah threw up his hands and watched Ella roar down his driveway, gravel kicking under her tyres.

Why was she upset? Micah replayed their conversation in his head, frowning. She'd told him Alta didn't like Thadie and he'd disagreed. He honestly didn't know how they'd gone from what he thought was a minor difference of opinion to her belting away from him.

Women. They were complicated characters.

Micah heard his name being called and spun round to see the twins hurtling across the lawn towards him, Thadie trailing behind them. He understood three-year-old boys. Sexy, complex woman? Not at all.

Micah dropped to the balls of his feet, opened up his arms and braced himself for the attack. As they connected with him, he gathered them up, tucked them under his arms and spun them around. They yelled their approval and, when he felt himself getting light-headed, stopped. They demanded more and, because he was a sucker, he did it again.

When he dropped them to their feet, he noticed two

hadidahs pecking at the grass on the far side of the lawn and suggested they try and catch the birds. They never would, but it would give him the chance to talk to his sister.

When they were out of earshot, Micah turned to Thadie. 'For someone who is getting married soon at a still-unknown venue, you are looking remarkably relaxed.'

Thadie raised her shoulders. 'Me worrying about it won't help. And I have a feeling we will find a venue.' Thadie tucked her hand into his elbow and rested her temple on his bicep. 'I like Ella, Micah.'

He knew she was fishing for more information on whether they were more than work colleagues, but he wasn't going to touch that comment with a barge pole. Yes, he liked Ella but she hadn't changed, and wasn't going to change, his mind about marriage and commitment.

As she'd slid behind the wheel earlier, he'd caught something in her eyes. Hurt and sadness... Had he let her down in some way? He couldn't think of what he'd said to make her feel like that. It couldn't be because Alta had come onto him and Ella was that insecure or petty. No, her pain went deeper than that...

And why did he care? She was leaving. They couldn't have a relationship because he didn't deserve one, but neither would he risk hurting her in any way.

But, damn, no woman had ever tempted him this quickly and this much.

Thadie tapped her sunglasses against her bicep and pulled her lower lip between her teeth. She glanced at

the twins, who were on their bellies trying to stealth-
ily approach the birds, and gestured to the bench underneath his favourite oak tree. 'Let's sit down for a
moment.'

He knew that tone of voice and recognised the look
on her face. She had something on her mind, was wres-
tling with a decision. They sat down on the bench and
he flung his arm around her shoulder. 'What's up?
How can I help?'

'I'm thinking of asking Alta to step down as my
bridesmaid.'

His eyebrows shot up. 'Okay, that wasn't what I expected you to say. Why?'

Thadie turned to face him. 'She's so negative,
Micah. Nothing is ever good enough for her and I'm
so sick of what she calls "constructive criticism". She
also doesn't like me,' Thadie added.

Huh. So Ella was right.

'If that's the way you feel, then boot her. But Clyde
might not like it,' Micah warned his sister. Alta was,
after all, Clyde's stepsister and brand manager.

'I've asked him to talk to Alta, to ask her to tone
down her attitude, but he hasn't, so he's left me with
no choice. I won't be miserable on my wedding day,'
Thadie replied, her tone fierce.

'No, that would be unacceptable. Fire her, and know
that you have our full support,' Micah assured her.

'I'll call her later,' Thadie said, grimacing. 'It's not
going to be a pleasant conversation. Alta can be quite
fiery.'

Micah kissed her head. 'My money is on you, kid.'

Across the lawn, the *hadidahs* took flight with their trademark indignant squawk and the twins rolled in the grass, laughing with complete abandon. 'Isn't that the best sound?' Thadie asked, her hand on her heart and her eyes misty with emotion.

'I remember you laughing like that,' Micah told her, kissing the top of her head. 'Good job on raising happy kids, sweetheart.'

And, talking about sweethearts, he needed to head across town and find out what had turned Ella from sweet to sad. He'd never get any work done this weekend if he didn't. Not that he would anyway, since thoughts of Ella were constantly front and centre and consistently distracting.

It had been two sentences—*She's harmless. You're overreacting*—but it had spun her off her axis, tilted her world. Ella paced her all but empty apartment, cursing herself. Those few words shouldn't have had the power to wound her. She should be able to shrug them off, let them go.

She had to get past the mental trauma of the past two months and come to terms with the fact that people weren't always going to agree with her, listen to her, take her seriously.

She understood it on an intellectual level but she couldn't make her stubborn heart see reason. Despite thinking she'd made progress in coming to terms with being accosted and then not believed, that tenacious organ was still sulking, still feeling battered and bruised. She knew that a large part of her trauma had to do with her dad not listening to her about calling an ambulance for her mum, and that experience, and the events of the past months, had created a psychological fog she was trying to find her way through.

But she couldn't keep feeling like this and reacting badly when a conversation didn't go her way. If she did, her life would be hell. Maybe, if those words hadn't come from Micah, she would've reacted more calmly. But they'd come from the mouth of a man she admired, respected…someone she liked.

A man she could, in another life and at another time, fall in love with.

Think, Ella, don't just feel. Be sensible.

Was there a chance she was confusing attraction with gratitude because he was the only person who believed her about what had happened with Pillay? Was she feeling indebted to him because he'd leapt into action and righted a wrong, acting like a modern-day knight?

No. While she was grateful for him for resolving her issues with Le Roux Events, she wouldn't have slept with him if she didn't feel something for him, if she wasn't crazy attracted to him. Ella rested her forearms along the back of the couch and dropped her head between her arms, feeling flustered and frustrated. She'd only met him a few days ago. Nobody should have this much effect on her so quickly! But, as she was coming to realise, Micah didn't do what people expected him to.

With most people he was startlingly suave and appealing, quick with a smile but with her he was differ-

ent. With her he occasionally discarded that cloak of
geniality and allowed himself to be mercurial, impulsive, occasionally grumpy, more real. He'd even opened
up a little: she knew that his butler was a father figure
to him, that he didn't like the person he'd been as a
teenager and that he'd do anything and everything for
his family. She knew that he was a brilliant, creative,
considerate lover and that he had a streak of integrity
a mile wide.

Despite only knowing him for a little less than a
week, she felt connected to him, as if he was an old
friend or a lover from a previous life. Ella pushed her
fingertips into her forehead, rolling her eyes and her
fanciful thoughts. Simply put, she liked him. In bed
and out. A lot.

A hell of a lot.

His opinion mattered to her. And she wanted hers to
matter to him. And she wanted to feel strong enough,
confident enough, to challenge him when she disagreed
with him. Not to argue or to be proved right, but self-
assured enough to defend her corner, as she knew he
would his.

This had very little to do with whether Alta liked
Thadie or not. It was about her own reaction to Micah
disagreeing with her and—God, this was hard to
admit—about the balance of power. Micah had most
of it. Not because he wanted it but because she lacked
the confidence to grab her share.

Oh, why was she even thinking like this, contem-
plating a life beyond the short time they had left together? She was over-thinking, over-analysing.

Overreacting.

Ella's head snapped up at the hard rap on her door and she frowned. Janie knew where she lived but her friend was out of town this weekend.

There was only one other person who had her address...

Ella stood and walked slowly over to her door, looking through the peephole just to make sure. She sighed, released the chain, flipped her locks and opened the door, leaning against the door frame.

'I thought you had work to do,' Ella told him, trying to sound bored.

'I do,' Micah replied. 'And it concerns you. Want to tell me why you stormed away earlier?'

'No.' It was a truthful answer because she didn't want to tell him. Kiss him, make love to him, sure. Talk about her hang-ups? No, thank you.

'Can I come in?' Micah asked, looking over her shoulder into the emptiness beyond.

She didn't want him to see her empty flat, to take in the bare, cold, white walls. Her flat was soulless, and she didn't want him to think she was too.

Before she could find the words to answer his question, Micah cupped her face in his hands and gently kissed her mouth. It was a soft kiss, an *I've got you* kiss, a kiss that brought tears to her eyes. Because she'd had so little tenderness for so long, it had the ability to drop her to her knees.

Micah dropped his hands, gripped her waist and quickly, with no effort at all, picked her up and walked her into the flat, kicking the door closed with his foot.

He put her back on her feet and looked around the open-plan lounge, diner and kitchen. When his eyes met hers, they were shot with steel.

'You told me that you are emigrating, so I'm presuming that you've been selling your stuff?'

'Yes.'

'That explains the empty flat. But if you've been sleeping on a mattress, I will lose it,' he warned her.

'I still have my bed,' Ella told him, trying to sound cool. God, he looked so big in this space, and he sucked up the air and energy.

He frowned at her and turned around in a slow circle before walking over to the fridge and yanking it open. Ella winced; it was mostly empty, as she'd planned to run down to the supermarket a block away to stock up on food for the weekend but hadn't got round to doing it. Her small freezer held nothing but a couple of ice trays.

Micah opened a few more cupboards, growing considerably more tense. Slamming a door shut, he shook his head and, without saying anything to her, stomped across her flat to open the door to her bedroom and disappeared inside. Ella frowned and followed him.

When she got there, he was lifting her small suitcase—the one she'd used on their trip to Clarens—onto her bed.

'What the hell are you doing, Micah?'

'I'm taking you home to Hadleigh House.'

He was? This was news to her.

'You don't have any food in this house, no furniture…you don't even have a TV for entertainment! You have a couch and a bed!' he stated, his tone grim.

She knew that; she lived here. 'I'm only buying what I need so I don't have to throw anything away when I leave. And it's only me, so a couch is more than adequate, and I have a laptop on which I can work or watch movies or listen to music,' Ella replied, bemused by his annoyance at the way she was living. 'I'm perfectly comfortable, Micah.'

'Well, I'm not, Ella! I'm not comfortable with any of this!' Micah stated, looking irritated. 'I'm not comfortable with how much I want you, how much I hate seeing you live like this.'

She wasn't living rough, for goodness' sake.

Micah pushed both his hands through his hair. 'And I'm sure as hell not comfortable with whatever it was that sent you flying away from Hadleigh like a bat out of hell.' He pointed a finger at her. 'And we are going to talk about that, by the way.'

God, she loved it when he sounded a little out of control, fractionally uncivilised.

'Come back to my place with me, El. Come and lie by the pool, eat great food prepared by an excellent chef, watch movies in our media room. I need to work, as I have quite a bit to do, but I won't get a damn thing done knowing you are here…'

Ella tipped her head to the side. He seemed genuinely stressed by her living here, surrounded by white walls and her few boxes. 'I'm not on the verge of homelessness, Micah.'

A look of pure frustration crossed his face. 'I know

that; I'm not that much of a snob,' he snapped. He held up his hands, annoyed and frustrated. 'I want you with me, okay? I want to know that you are around, that I can find you when I'm done with work. I want us to spend time together.'

Aw...

'And when we make love—and we will, often— I'd prefer to do it in my enormous bed, where we have space to move.'

Oh, that did sound amazing. Ella rubbed the back of her neck. But should she spend the rest of the weekend with him? She was tempted, of course she was—who wouldn't want to spend time with Micah in his glorious house?—but, given that she was a conflicted mess of too-hard-to-handle emotions, *should* she? It was one thing to have a one-night stand, another to spend hours with him, lounging around, eating his food, drinking his wine, swimming in his pool. Exploring his delicious body...

He'd already turned her world upside down. How would she be after spending concentrated time with him?

She was just making it harder to leave him, to say goodbye. But leave she would, so why not make a couple of memories she could hold on to? Decisions, decisions...

She nodded. 'Okay, I'll spend the weekend with you.'

Ella turned back to her cupboard to grab some clothes but Micah's hand on her arm kept her in place. 'Not so fast, sweetheart. What happened earlier?'

She wrinkled her nose, thinking of what to say, how to explain.

'It doesn't matter,' she told him.

'It does to me.'

Micah walked to the nearest wall, leaned his shoulder into it and crossed his ankles. He didn't push her to speak, just waited her out. And she knew that he would stand there until she told him what had upset her earlier.

She couldn't think of an excuse and she wouldn't make up a story. So that meant telling him the truth. As much as she could. But would he understand? Could she trust him with this?

Ella sat down on the edge of her bed and placed her hands down beside her, her fingers digging into the fabric of her cotton bed cover. 'As I said, my mum died when I was sixteen on the most stunning summer's day. A day much like this one, actually.'

Micah didn't drop his eyes from hers, neither did he speak, so she carried on. 'My mum liked to drink at lunchtime over the weekends and she had a couple of G&Ts that day. She stood up from the lunch table and, basically, her legs crumpled. She dropped like a stone. I rushed around the table and she was muttering, speaking but making no sense.'

Ella rubbed her fingertips across her forehead. 'I knew, at that moment, that there was something wrong with her. I told my dad to call an ambulance but he said no, that she was drunk—he hated her drinking—and that she just needed to sleep it off. I knew she wasn't drunk, but he wouldn't budge. I screamed, yelled, pleaded and, when I tried to call for an ambulance on my phone, he pulled it out of my hands. He put her to bed to sleep it off.'

'But she wasn't drunk.'

'She died later that afternoon, a few hours after she collapsed.' Ella shook her head. 'She had a massive brain bleed, some sort of stroke. Apparently, the worst thing to do when that happens is to go to sleep.'

Micah didn't issue any platitudes, didn't fuss. She appreciated that. 'Is that why you and your dad don't speak, because he didn't call an ambulance?'

'I was upset that he didn't call an ambulance—still am—but I've never blamed him for her death. Not really. How could I when he blamed himself? He fell apart so completely when she died,' she explained. She shrugged. 'I don't know why he's cut me out of his life. Maybe it's because he feels guilty, maybe I remind him too much of her. Maybe it's because he wishes I'd died, not her.'

Micah's eyes widened in horror. 'El, don't say that!'

Pain spiked and flared. 'Why not? He doesn't want anything to do with me and doesn't care what happens to me.'

She heard her voice rising and winced. It was time to pull back, to take control of her emotions. After taking a few deep breaths, she spoke again, and was happy to hear her voice sounded normal. 'All I know is that I lost two parents that day. Because my dad didn't believe me and, having recently experienced being disbelieved and diminished, I'm currently super-sensitive when I think my opinion is being dismissed.'

He nodded. 'And you thought I did that when we were talking about Alta and Thadie?'

She nodded. She fought the urge to apologise for being silly, to mock her feelings. And she prayed that he wouldn't either.

'I'm sorry.'

It was a straightforward apology, and she saw the sincerity in his eyes. Tension flowed out of her body and her shoulders dropped from just below her ears.

After a few seconds of silence, Micah rubbed the back of her neck. 'Talking of your recent past…'

Oh, God, where was he going with this?

'Were you okay with everything we did in Clarens? I think you had a good time but I just want to make sure that you are completely okay. Maybe I was too demanding, maybe you needed me to be—'

'You… It was *perfect*, Micah,' Ella rushed to reassure him, touched that he'd asked. She stood up to walk over to him and placed a hand on his chest, needing to feel connected to him.

'I was lucky, so lucky. I spoke to a therapist after it happened and I've worked through it. You gave me exactly what I needed, Micah, a fantastic experience. I don't have any hang-ups about sex, I promise you. Even before I spoke to my therapist, I never equated what he did to me with sex. It was about power and control.'

He gently brushed her hair back from her forehead. 'You didn't deserve that, Ella.'

'No, I didn't.'

Micah's thumb skated over her cheekbone. 'If I ever

do something, make you feel something that…well…
that reminds you, will you tell me?'

That he'd even thought to make that offer heated Ella's blood and made her heart flutter. Kind, gruff, occasionally edgy…now she could add 'sweet' to her list
of descriptors for Micah she had running in her head.

Because he still looked worried, and because she
wanted to prove to him that there was no link between
how he made her feel and Pillay's actions, Ella linked
her arms around Micah's neck and placed her lips on
his. There had been too much talking and not enough
kissing, in her opinion.

She felt Micah's hesitation, knew that he was de-
bating whether to push for more information, so she
pulled his bottom lip between hers and nibbled softly.
He sighed and she slipped her tongue between his
open lips, seeking his. Ella wound her tongue around
his, and his fingertips pressed into the skin above her
knees. Micah held her against his body, so tightly that
the buttons of his shirt dug into her chest. One arm
banded around her, and his other hand came up to cup
her head, holding it in place as he took their kiss deeper
to hot, undiscovered depths.

Her hands skated up and down his sides, over his
broad back, her fingers playing in his hair. She touched
his jaw and ran her hand down the cords of his neck,
down his chest. She couldn't get enough of him and
she couldn't wait, not one second longer, to have him
have her again.

In every delightful way possible.

Forcing herself to wrench her mouth off his, she grabbed his hand and tugged him back to the bed.

Lying down next to her, Micah's fingers danced over her clavicle before coming to cover her breast. Ella arched into his hand and groaned. She flung her thigh over his hip and went to work on the buttons of his shirt, ripping some in her frustration to get to his bare skin.

Micah's hand on her thigh tightened and he pulled away from her mouth to haul in a couple of deep breaths.

Ella frowned. 'Why did you stop? What's the problem?'

His eyes blazed with blue fire. 'The problem is that I'm trying to slow this down because I am this far—' he lifted his hand to show her an inch-wide space between his thumb and index finger '—from ripping your clothes off and plunging inside you.'

Ella fumbled for the zip on her jumpsuit. 'Why don't you do just that?'

Micah held her eyes for a moment, nodded and went on to do exactly what he'd said.

CHAPTER NINE

HOPING NOT TO wake Ella, who slept on the pool lounger under the shade of a huge umbrella, Micah quietly slipped into his pool and started to swim, pulling through the water silently and effortlessly. Every time he turned his head, he caught a glimpse of the lounger where Ella slept and told himself that he should let her sleep, that he needed to exercise, that he couldn't wake her up by kissing her instep, dragging his tongue up the inside of her calf, nibbling her knee.

In the four hours he'd spent in his office, he'd managed to complete what he called his 'zombie work'—tasks he could accomplish without needing much brain power or concentration. Most of his focus was on what Ella had told him, and now and again he had to push aside the images of her being manhandled, to breathe through his anger. He had to remind himself, often, that she hadn't been hurt, that things hadn't gone that far…

She was right: she'd been lucky. But it should never have happened in the first place.

He was astounded at how much Ella had had to deal with and how well she was handling the events of the past few months, especially since the actions of his employees dug into an old, personal wound. She'd already had issues with not being believed, but being sexually accosted and then having her allegations dismissed and derided must've rocked her world.

Must be still rocking her world. No one recovered from that sort of trauma quickly. And she'd done it alone. He'd heard her mention a Janie from work and, while it sounded as if they were friends, he didn't know if they were close enough for Ella to confide in her. He could be wrong but he suspected that Ella walked through the world solo, and that was a dark and desperately lonely path.

Even at his lowest points, he always had Jago standing behind him. He knew that his twin would never let him down, would always be at his side and would help him slay any and all dragons. Now that she was an adult, Micah also had Thadie's full support, and Jabu had been the rock he'd rested on many times throughout his life. Ella didn't have anyone.

The thought made him want to weep. And howl. And fix...

She'd crawled under his skin and was banging on the door to his disused, mangled heart. And he wasn't the only one to realise the impact she'd made in such a short time. Thadie had also noticed. Why else would she tell him she liked one of their many employees? No, it was Thadie's way of giving him her blessing, of telling him she approved.

After lunch, when Ella had gone upstairs to change into a swimsuit, Jabu had informed him he'd set up the lounger by the pool for Ella and that he intended to make her as comfortable as possible, supplying her with water and fruit. He'd even taken a quick drive to Thadie's house and borrowed a couple of her magazines in case Ella wanted them.

Leaving the premises to borrow magazines was a pretty big deal, and he'd asked Jabu why he was going the extra mile.

Jabu had sent him a steady look. 'How many people offer their hand to a butler and say, with complete sincerity, how happy she is to meet me? No one, that's how many.'

Right. Ella had Mkulu's seal of approval. Not that she needed it, because their relationship wasn't going anywhere! How many times would he have to repeat that before it started sinking into his suddenly stubborn brain?

Micah felt a small hand grip his ankle and he whirled around to see Ella hanging on to the side of the deep end of the pool, her hair off her face brown and glossy. She gave him an open and lovely smile. It was obvious that she had no idea he'd spent the last ten minutes fantasising about how good it would feel to rearrange Pillay's handsome features.

He planted his feet on the bottom of the pool and pushed his hair off his face. 'Did you have a good nap?'

'Mmm,' Ella said, moving towards him, wrapping her arms around his neck and her legs around his waist. She felt so good in his arms, so feminine. A wave of protectiveness rose within him; she was his to protect.

His to keep. His to love…

For the next week or so at least.

Confused by the unfamiliar emotions washing through him, Micah dipped his head and covered her mouth with his, smiling as she sunk into him, falling into the kiss. Passion flared between them, as hot and fiery as a rocket launch. He'd never felt this way before. Sure, he'd felt desire, but as soon as that was sated he lost interest. But, with Ella, she fired up his mind and his heart, as well as his body.

It was a potent combination...

Ella pulled back from his mouth to drop little kisses along his jawline, slowly meandering her way to his ear. She kissed the spot where his neck met his ear before whispering directly in his ear, 'Let's go upstairs and roll around in your bed.'

He loved the fact that she was so forthright and had no qualms about telling, or showing, how much she wanted him.

'I can't wait that long,' Micah told her, his hand coming up to cover her breast. He dragged his thumb over her nipple and Ella sighed. A second later she stiffened and he felt her legs releasing their grip around his waist.

'What's the problem?' Micah asked, frowning.

'I am.'

Hearing that voice, Micah cursed. Under the water, he clenched his fists. He told himself to find his implacable expression and, when he thought he had it, he slowly turned around.

His stepmother stood between the loungers and the pool, dressed in a pistachio jumpsuit, three-inch heels and a gold chain as thick as his finger. She wore braids today, and she'd pulled them back from her face, highlighting those world-famous cheekbones. She was in her fifties now but she could still pass for a woman twenty years younger.

'Jabu isn't in the house,' Liyana stated, her eyes locked on his. So far, she hadn't even acknowledged Ella's presence.

'It's his night off,' Micah told her, widening his stance and folding his arms. He lifted his eyebrows.

'Jago?' Liyana demanded.

'He's out for the evening,' Micah replied, trying to keep the impatience out of his voice.

This was his stepmother, for God's sake, a woman who'd been around for most of his life. How much longer were they going to keep up this cold war? It was so stupid and it didn't serve any purpose. But he was stubborn and she was stubborn…

She was also looking stressed, Micah decided. On closer inspection, the grooves next to her mouth seemed deeper, the frown between her eyebrows wider. Liyana was seriously tense, upset about something. Thadie's wedding problems? Maybe. Whatever it was, she was worried enough to come across from her house to find him. Well, to find Jabu and give him a message…

Micah swiftly crossed to the wall, hauled himself out in one easy movement and walked around the pool to stand a few feet from Liyana. Out of the corner of his eye, he saw Ella holding out a towel and he took it, nodding his thanks.

'I'll see you inside,' Ella said softly as he wound the towel around his hips.

He shook his head and pointed to the lounger, silently asking her to stay. If they had company, there was a good chance that they'd rein in their tempers and behave themselves. Liyana hated making a scene. Ella wrapped her sarong around her waist and sat down on the edge of the lounger. Just seeing her there made him feel stronger, more in control. Better.

What was she doing to him? Why did she have this effect on him?

Turning his attention back to Liyana, he spoke again. 'I can see that you are upset, Liyana. And the fact that you are still here tells me that you have something to say. What is it?'

Liyana played with the solid gold bracelet on her arm. 'I don't talk to Brianna's mother any more. I haven't since…' She trailed off, looking away.

Yes, he got it. Since the night he'd run out of the house.

'But Kate and I do have mutual friends, as the society we keep is a very small one,' Liyana continued.

Micah clenched his fists, trying to keep his temper. His stepmother was a complete snob and considered herself Johannesburg and African royalty. If you wanted to be friends with Liyana Le Roux, you had to be either stupendously rich, famous or powerful. Preferably all three.

Liyana hauled in a deep breath and he noticed that she seemed genuinely upset. 'I have it on good authority that Brianna has a serious respiratory infection.

She's not responding to the antibiotics and they don't think she's going to make it.'

A cold hand encircled Micah's heart and pushed ice into his veins.

'Kate is preparing herself for the worst.'

Micah gripped the bridge of his nose with his thumb and index finger. 'Do they still have a DNR policy in place?' After Brianna's father, Phil, died he'd heard that Kate had put a Do Not Resuscitate order in place. In essence, it said that if Brianna had a heart attack the staff would not resuscitate her.

Liyana nodded. 'Yes. Kate won't remove her feeding tube but she did put the DNR in place.'

Micah hunched his shoulders. He didn't know what to say or how to act. He never did. Eventually, he spoke again. 'Thanks for coming to tell me. Will you let me know if…?'

Liyana nodded, opened her mouth to say something else and shook her head. Then she ducked her head and briskly strode away, back to her house and her life as Theo's rich widow and society maven.

Was it wrong to wish that the infection would take Brianna, that she'd just slip away? He'd hoped, for years and years, that she'd recover—medical miracles did happen, after all. But, as he'd aged, he'd prayed that she'd be released from the space she occupied between life and death.

It was no place for someone to live, especially someone as vibrant as Brianna.

Micah felt Ella's hand rubbing his back, then she linked her fingers with his and led him to the veranda.

He sat down on the first piece of furniture he encountered, a four-seater couch, spread his legs and dropped his head, drops of pool water dotting the non-slip tiles.

He heard Ella opening the door to the fridge behind the bar, the snap of a beer bottle cap being removed and then he felt the cold bottle against his bicep.

He took it, downed half the bottle and rested the icy glass against his forehead. Ella sat down next to him, her small shoulder pressing into his upper arm.

She sat there silently, offering him comfort, making no demands for an explanation. But he wanted to tell her, wanted to shine a spotlight on the darkest, scariest time of his life. Somehow, though he knew not how, she'd crow-barred her way into his life, opening doors that were long closed.

'That was Liyana,' he explained, sitting up.

'I gathered,' Ella quietly responded. 'She's stunningly beautiful.'

'She's also stunningly high maintenance. We don't talk,' Micah admitted. 'That was the most we've spoken in months, maybe years.'

Ella took a sip from her water bottle and didn't ask the obvious follow-up question: Why? She'd pulled on her tank top but her pretty feet remained bare. He could turn and face her, kiss her until he forgot about Liyana's news, until he was lost in her. But while that appealed—and always would, he suspected—his urge to unburden himself was stronger than his desire.

Another first.

'Liyana married my dad six weeks after my mum died. I don't know if they fell in love quickly or whether they were having an affair before my mum passed away. It's not something I need an answer to.'

He went on to explain that his father had had a terrible temper, that he'd been incredibly volatile and that, while Jago had tried to keep the peace, or at least tried to avoid the eruptions, he'd run head-first into the volcano. He'd argued, fought and bucked the system.

'I was a nightmare child,' he confessed.

'You were angry and grieving and it doesn't sound like you were given the time and space to mourn your mum. It sounds like your feelings were dismissed and you were forced to accept the status quo.' Ella bumped his shoulder. 'I don't think you've accepted the status quo a day in your life, Le Roux.'

That was true. It was in his nature to question, to dissect. He rarely took anything at face value.

Ella's hand on his thigh, a gentle squeeze, was her silent way of telling him to continue. 'The older I got, the more out of control I became. I was the ultimate rich-boy rebel.'

He stopped, not sure if he could carry on. If he told her about The Incident, there would be no going back. He would be sharing with her, someone who was little more than a stranger the event that had defined his life. How would she react? Would she say something trite, or go into a deep psychological analysis? He didn't want either, he just wanted her to listen, to be on his side, to look at him kindly.

He didn't know if she would.

'Who's Brianna, Micah? And why is she on a feeding tube?'

Micah drained his beer, put the bottle on the table next to him and gripped her hand in his. 'She was my, *our*, oldest friend. Her parents were my parents' best friends and we grew up together. She loved me.'

'As a sister or as a lover?'

'Initially, as a sister, but then as we hit our late teens it was obvious that she was in love with me. I didn't love her like that but, being the young, spoiled bastard I was, I didn't have any problem with stringing her along. I'd make out with her, then move on to the next girl. I later learned she spent many nights crying over me. I'm not proud of that.

'But she was the person that I could always talk to about everything. She knew about my relationship with Theo and Liyana, how lost and unloved I felt. Jago was the oldest, and perfect, you know? Bright and sporty, and he worked the system rather than bucking it. Thadie was a ray of sunshine, sweet and lovely. I was the middle child who caused grief. I wasn't really necessary.'

Ella made a sound in her throat that sounded like disagreement. He stared out at the row of oak trees at the bottom of the garden. He told her about the argument with his dad and Liyana, that Theo's punch had broken his nose and his need to get out of the house. He explained that he'd called Brianna, had told her that he was heading for a sketchy bar, that he was going to get wasted and stoned.

'She knew where I was going. I'd told her about the place before. She hated me going there because it was a bad area...the bar was filled with lowlifes and known for vicious fights. At the time, I guess I felt at home there.'

Ella rested her temple on his shoulder. *'Micah.'*

'She told me not to go…begged me to come to her place instead. I cut the call but she kept calling, texting, leaving voice messages. I didn't read or listen to them, I just wanted to be alone. She blew up my phone and I switched it off.'

'Did she follow you?'

'Yeah. She wasn't an experienced driver and hated driving at night. She had a head-on collision, which resulted in severe neurological brain damage. She's been in a permanent vegetative state since she was eighteen years old.'

Ella half-turned to face him, placed her forehead on the ball of his shoulder and closed her eyes. 'God, that's horrible.'

Needing to tell her everything, Micah explained how his parents had blamed him for the accident, that they hadn't spoken to him for two years, and that Brianna's parents had sued him but the court case had ultimately been dismissed. That, if not for him, Brianna would likely be married by now, probably with a heap of kids.

Ella scooted backwards so that she could look at his face without tipping her head back. 'You blame yourself,' she said.

'My actions led to her spending her life in a hospital bed, unresponsive,' Micah stated.

Ella frowned at him. 'No, your actions led to your dad punching you—which is unforgivable, in my view.

No matter the circumstances, no parent should hit a child, *ever*.' She saw that he was about to speak and shook her head. 'Don't even try and say you deserved it, Micah, I won't accept it. Your father was the adult in the room and him punching you is indefensible.'

Jago had told him that before—so had the therapist—but the words seemed to resonate today, when he heard them from Ella's lips. He did not doubt that he'd been revolting, but Theo punching him really *had* been unacceptable...

'As for Brianna, it was her choice to follow you to a bad area in town and to drive at night when she wasn't experienced. She was reckless, Micah, and very foolish.'

'But...'

Ella shook her head. 'I'm not done. Your parents should've stood by you, not isolated and ignored you. They could've hated what you did but still loved you.'

Hated what...? 'Sorry, say that again?'

'I said that Theo and Liyana could've hated your actions but still loved and supported *you*.'

That. That made sense. He'd done something ridiculously reckless and stupid, had been out of control and irresponsible, but his father and stepmother had made him feel rotten to the core, as if he deserved no love and support.

For the first time, Micah could look back and see the boy he'd been—lonely, lost and desperate to feel connected to his family. Theo and Liyana hadn't known how to handle his in-your-face personality and, instead of talking calmly to him, rationalising as Jabu had, they'd screamed, shouted and tried to impose their will on him.

'And I suppose you have this notion that, because you were the reason Brianna jumped into her car and had an accident, you now have to atone for your sins by solving the world's problems or, at the very least, the Le Rouxs' problems?'

Well, yeah. He darted a look at her and she lifted her eyebrows, waiting for his response. What else could he do but nod?

'And you believe that, because Brianna can't have a life, neither can you?'

'I have a life!' Micah protested.

Ella rolled her eyes. 'You live in the shallows, Micah. You don't fall in love, you don't commit... I presume you have no intention of marrying and having children?' Ella demanded.

'I don't,' he admitted.

'Okay, I'm not going to tell you how nonsensical that is—' except that she just had '—but I'm going to ask you one question, just one.'

Micah tensed.

'What would change for Brianna if you fell in love, married, had kids?'

He didn't understand her question. 'What do you mean?'

She placed her hand on his cheek. 'Would Brianna's condition improve?'

'Brianna is never going to wake up,' Micah said coldly.

'And that's my point, Micah,' Ella gently told him.

'Whether you live your life fully or skate along the surface, nothing is going to change for Brianna. She won't know, she'll *never* know. You are punishing yourself when you are not to blame for her accident, and your denying yourself happiness will never change Brianna's condition. Micah, don't you see? You're also in a coma, but yours is an emotional one, and you placed yourself in it. It serves no purpose but to feed your guilt.'

Ella leaned forward, placed her lips on his cheek and then pulled back. 'I'm sorry about Brianna, Micah, I am. But you're a good man who deserves to be happy. You've punished yourself long enough. Enough, now.'

Micah watched, his brain whirling as she stood up and walked into the house, her hips swaying. When she disappeared, he stood up and went to the bar fridge to get himself another beer, idly popping the top. He sipped and looked onto the rose garden, the one his mum had loved so much.

He was an adult and, for the first time in his life, could look back on the child and teenager he'd been without wincing and cringing. Theo had been a bully and had had no idea how to be a dad, and Liyana had been a young herself, not yet twenty-four when she'd met and married his much older dad. What had she known about raising twin boys and dealing with Theo's volcanic personality?

Ella was right—his father punching him had been unforgivable. No matter how badly behaved he'd been, he hadn't deserved to get his nose broken.

He'd been a lonely, lost and rebellious kid with too

much money and freedom and not enough love. He'd made some stupid decisions but Ella had nailed it—it wasn't his fault that Brianna had followed him to that pub. That had been her decision; he'd never asked her to.

His parents, and her parents, shouldn't have laid all the blame at his door. But when the unimaginable happened people needed a place to put their anger. He'd been disliked, misunderstood and difficult, and it was easier to blame him than to apportion any blame to the angelic-looking girl being kept alive by a feeding tube.

He got it; he did.

You're also in a coma, but yours is an emotional one...

Ella was correct—he was. And he was the only person who could pull himself out of it, to start to live again properly and fully. And he wanted to do that with Ella.

He tightened his grip on his bottle, wondering if he was just confusing lust and gratitude with a need for permanence, to create the family he'd always wanted. Was he imagining himself in love with her—or something close—because she'd cracked open some emotional doors and made him look at things differently?

In the space of a few short days, she'd changed his life but, bombarded with emotion, he didn't know what was real or false any more, what was true and lasting or ephemeral.

Before he said something he couldn't take back, before he did anything that he couldn't unravel, he needed to make sure of his feelings.

Very sure.

* * *

Ella went upstairs and walked into Micah's shower, turning the powerful jets to cool. She stripped off her clothes and stepped under the spray. When the first blast of water hit her skin, she started to cry.

So much made sense now, things she hadn't understood were falling into place. Micah wasn't meant to be alone, he had too much to give, but he'd taken himself away and made himself emotionally unavailable because he felt as though he didn't deserve to be loved, to be in love.

He was a guy who took responsibility, too much of it. Yes, he'd been a stupid kid, but his girlfriend had chosen to run to Micah's rescue—out of love, friendship, a need to protect and save…who knew? The result of that decision had been catastrophic but Micah wasn't to blame…and how dared his and her parents do that to an already messed up kid?

Despite the life blows he'd been dealt as a young adult, he'd managed to become an incredible man. So many kids would've lost themselves in alcohol or drugs, but Micah had just absorbed the blows, got an education, become a successful businessman and looked after his family. He was amazing, she thought, tears mingling with the shower spray. How was she going to stop herself from falling in love with him now?

How was she going to leave?

Ella heard the shower door opening but didn't turn around, not wanting Micah to see her red eyes. She felt his arms encircle her waist and he pulled her back and touched his lips to her hair. His big body enveloped her and, for the first time since she'd been sixteen, she felt completely safe. He'd stand between her and the world; he was that type of guy.

A guy she needed, enjoyed, possibly loved. *Probably* loved.

Micah's big hands came up to cup her breasts and his thumbs brushed over her nipples. Ella arched her back, pushing into his touch. She loved the way he could pull her out of the mental and into the physical, how he managed to stop time in its tracks.

Micah pulled her hair to the side and ran his tongue up her neck, then back down again and across her shoulder, gently nipping it. His erection pushed against her bottom and lower back, hard and insistent, but Micah didn't turn her around, instead choosing to slide his hand over her ribs and down her stomach, flirting with the small triangle down below. Placing her hand on top of his, she guided his fingers between her folds, releasing a gasp when he hit her sweet spot.

He knew exactly how to touch her, when to slow down, when to speed up. When to retreat, when to push her harder. Tears forgotten, Ella arched into his hand, needing the amazing orgasm only he could give her.

She reached back and hooked her arm around his neck, turning her head to find his warm lips, his seeking tongue. They kissed like that for minutes, years, millennia, wanting to spin out this moment. But, when Ella pushed her hips back and stood on her tiptoes so that Micah could slide his finger inside her, he spun her round and captured her mouth in a kiss designed to shatter stars. Without releasing her mouth, he boosted her up his body, resting her back against the wall.

'Wrap your legs around me and hold on,' Micah told her, his voice guttural with need.

Ella did as he commanded and he positioned himself to enter her but pulled back at the last second, cursing. 'Condom,' he muttered, pulling a foil packet off the shelf to his right.

With her feet back on the floor, she watched him open the packet, jumpy with impatience.

"Hurry up, Micah, I'm dying here…"

She'd barely finished her sentence when Micah pushed inside her, filling her completely. The shower wall was cool against her back, and water droplets from the shower peppered her head, but all she cared about was that Micah was kissing her, rocking her to new heights.

Ella felt herself skimming along the face of a huge wave, wondering when she'd crash. Whenever she thought she would, Micah would slow down, pull back, and the wave would die just a little. But he'd build her up again to the point she was screaming, begging for him to let her tumble.

He surged once, then again, and he hit a spot deep inside her. Ella screamed in pleasure and she was hit from all sides by sensation…

She heard Micah's shout and felt as he tightened his grip on her hips, his release pulsing deep inside her. It was enough to make her come again. Smaller this time, but no less intense.

As their heart rates slowed down, Micah stepped

back and held her steady as her feet hit the floor. He pulled her into his arms and held her close, his face buried in her neck. After a while, Micah turned the shower off, tossed his condom and led her, naked and soaking, to his bed.

CHAPTER TEN

THE NEXT MORNING Ella and Micah came downstairs to find Jabu laying two places at the end of the sixteen-seater wooden dining table on the veranda. It was another stunning day, hot and sunny, and the sky was a deep blue.

She was going to miss days like this when she left South Africa, she thought, wincing at the sharp pang somewhere around her heart. She greeted Jabu and, when he handed her a mug of coffee, she gave him her biggest smile. 'You're an angel, thank you.'

Jabu had no idea how much she needed caffeine after she'd spent most of the night being expertly loved by Micah. Or, judging by the twinkle in his eyes, maybe he did. Ella blushed. God, it was like trying to sneak out of your boyfriend's house after staying the night and finding his father standing at the front door.

'Morning, Mkulu,' Micah said, squeezing Jabu's shoulder. Micah, she noticed with amusement, had to pour his own coffee from the carafe on the tray.

'What would you like for breakfast?' Jabu asked

her as he gently eased two gorgeous white roses into a slender vase.

Ella didn't feel comfortable asking the elderly man to cook for her, especially on a Sunday. But she was starving, so what would be easy to prepare and would require no effort? 'Cereal would be great, thanks.'

She saw disappointment flash across Jabu's face. He *wanted* to cook, she realised. He wanted to do something for them. Not because he had to, not because it was his job, but because he adored Micah and seemed to take pleasure in looking after him. Ella held up her hand. 'Actually, I'm really hungry and cereal isn't going to make a dent. What do you suggest, Mr Mkhize?'

Her use of his surname, the respect she showed, pleased him. 'Please call me Jabu. I have some smoked salmon in the fridge, some organic duck eggs, home-churned butter. What about smoked salmon, a poached egg and hollandaise sauce on a bagel?'

Her mouth started to water and her taste buds tingled. 'That would be amazing, thank you.'

Jabu nodded regally and walked into the house with a spring in his step. As soon as he was out of sight, Micah swiped his mouth over hers. 'Thank you for that. If I was here on my own, he probably would've tossed a piece of stale bread at me.'

'Nonsense,' Ella briskly told him. 'He adores you and just wants to look after you.'

'You're a wise woman,' Micah told her, kissing the tip of her nose before stepping away to look at the Sunday newspapers that Jabu had placed on the coffee table behind her. Micah's voice had held more depth of feeling than a comment about breakfast required, and Ella knew he wasn't talking about her observations about Jabu but referring to what she'd said last night. She looked at him, sitting on the couch and reading the headlines, and her heart triple-thumped in her chest. He wore a red T-shirt, plain black board shorts, his feet were bare and he looked younger than he had yesterday. Lighter.

After making love this morning, she'd touched his cheek and asked him how he was feeling. He'd smiled, low and slow, and gently asked if they could take the day for themselves, if they could lock out the past and the future and just enjoy being together. Thinking they both could do with an easy, stress-free day, she nodded. His gentle 'thank you kiss' had led to her straddling him and rocking them to another orgasm.

It was a miracle that she could still walk and talk.

Taking her coffee, Ella walked to the steps that led down to the pool and looked over the garden. She still thought Hadleigh House would be the perfect place for a wedding—rich and sumptuous, completely lovely.

A country house wedding… That sparked a memory.

Spinning round, she walked back over to where Micah was sitting and saw a black tablet, one of many she'd seen scattered throughout the house. The tablets, Micah had told her, ran a programme that controlled the alarm, lights, temperature and everything else in the house.

She picked it up and waved it under Micah's nose. 'Can I use this to access the Internet?' she asked.

Micah nodded. 'Sure.'

She switched it on, did a general search, didn't find anything and tried another route. After ten minutes she found the article she'd remembered.

The Grand Old Lady is Getting a Makeover...

The owner of one of Johannesburg's oldest mansions has caused controversy by gutting the inside of his newly inherited mansion and knocking down the non-load-bearing walls of the historic home without consulting the authorities trusted with preserving old buildings. The walls of the once-famous Cathcart House ballroom, its three reception rooms and dining room have been knocked down to form an extensive open-plan living space, much to the horror of architectural historians.

The owner of the property, Mr Samuel Dobson, has agreed to suspend the renovation of the historical home, but sources close to Mr Dobson tell us that the lack of progress is due to Dobson's financial issues and not because he has any interest in maintaining the historic importance of Cathcart House...

Ella did a picture search for Cathcart House and scrolled through the many photographs of the property. The gardens, she established, had been a showpiece even back in the late eighteen-eighties, a few years after the house had been built. As per an arrangement made by a previous Cathcart in the nineteen-nineties, the gardens were maintained by the local gardening club, and the club was host to a rather important flower show in the spring.

Beautiful gardens, a vast space indoor space that could be used as a wedding reception venue, close to the church... Cathcart House could possibly, with a little imagination and some cash, be the perfect venue for Thadie's wedding.

'Micah?'

Micah lifted his head and sent her that warm, soft smile that liquefied her organs. It was a 'I'm happy you're here' smile...a 'I like seeing you in my home' smile.

'Another pretty dress, sweetheart.'

Ella looked down at her cheap-as-chips dress, a Boho-inspired loose cotton shift that ended above her knees. It wasn't designer, or anywhere close, but he didn't seem to care. 'Thanks.'

He stood up to pour more coffee into his mug. He looked down at her screen and lifted his eyebrows. 'Why are you looking at pictures of Cathcart House?' he asked. 'Do you want more coffee, by the way?'

Ella shook her head, glancing at the tablet screen. 'Do you know it?'

'I know of it. A friend of mine...well, someone I went to school with...owns it.'

'Really?'

Micah sat down again and leaned back, looking relaxed. 'He's the last in a very long line of Dobsons to live in the house. They are a very old, very well-known Johannesburg family. There was a dust-up a couple of months ago because he did some insensitive renovations to the place, if I remember correctly. I know a property consortium showed some interest in acquiring it.'

'Were you part of that consortium?' Ella asked. Le Roux International had interests in the property sector so it was a fair question.

'No, we don't buy properties with partners, El. Or, if we do, it's multi-billion-dollar projects, like malls or hotel chains.'

Right, a Victorian mansion in Johannesburg was small fish for him. The mind boggled.

'Why are you asking about Dobson's house?' Micah asked.

Ella took a deep breath and tossed the suggestion out there, hoping Micah was open-minded enough to consider the idea. 'Thadie said that she'd love to have a garden wedding, that she wanted to be married at home. She can't, but I'm thinking that many another Victorian mansion would work just as well?' She gestured to the tablet she'd placed on the table. 'The photos online show that it has potential to host a large wedding, it has an award-winning garden and, because of those renovations, it now has a huge space on the ground floor. The guests wouldn't have to change any of their accommodation arrangements, and it's actually closer to the church than this house is.'

Micah looked thoughtful. 'I'm not sure, sweetheart. It sounds like a hell of a stretch.'

She felt deep down in her gut that Cathcart House

was the answer to all of their prayers. It was time to
use Micah's contacts and his status as one of the city's
best-known businesspeople.

'Would you be able to get hold of him, ask him if
he'd be interested in hiring out the mansion? Maybe
see if we could take a peek to see if it's suitable?'

Micah rubbed the back of his neck, his expression
pensive. Then he picked up his phone, made a few calls
and within ten minutes secured them a late-afternoon
viewing of Cathcart House for the following Sunday.

There were huge benefits to being a powerful billionaire, Ella decided as Jabu walked into the entertainment area carrying a silver tray loaded with food.

A week later, Ella instantly fell in love with Cathcart
House. She loved its gardens, bigger even than those at
Hadleigh House and, although she'd never admit this to
Micah, prettier too. The house looked as if it belonged
in the Cape, a frothy behemoth of Cape Dutch gables,
tall brick chimneys and a wide, wraparound veranda.
Inside she was grateful to see that Samuel Dobson had
left the entrance hall alone, which had a grand Bur-
mese teak staircase running up the middle of the vast
space before wrapping round to a gallery.

The downstairs area was a massive, cavernous and
echoing interior space. Dobson had replaced the centu-
ries-old wooden doors and windows with handcrafted,
wooden bi-fold doors that opened to the veranda which
overlooked the two-acre garden.

Upstairs, the magnificent bedrooms—still fur-
nished—had been left untouched, with every room

boasting a fireplace and some sporting Victorian tiles and fine, beautifully carved wooden mantelpieces. All the floors upstairs were Oregon pine, badly in need of waxing and treating. The door handles and light switches were brass and, she was sure, made for the house.

It would be, with some money thrown at it, a perfect wedding venue, Ella thought, wandering through the downstairs area on her own. Micah and Samuel were in conversation, no doubt reminiscing about their school days, Samuel having been a year or two ahead of Micah at an elite boarding school somewhere in the KwaZulu Natal Midlands.

Ella was glad to have Samuel's eyes off her for a while; she'd felt as if he was undressing her every time he looked at her, and when she asked him a question he'd replied to her breasts. He made her skin crawl.

Overreacting, Yeung? Maybe. She had a habit of doing that… But she just didn't like Samuel. At all.

Ella turned her attention back to the building. The gardens were spectacular and, were she planning Thadie's wedding, she wouldn't change much. She'd give the veranda a quick lick of paint and wrap the columns with fairy lights. There would be a string quartet in the hall to welcome the guests, and she'd cover the ripped-out ceiling with swathes of white cloth, behind which would be more fairy lights. She paced the area out and established that there would be enough room for all the tables plus a band and a big dance floor. Dobson had done the house no favours by ripping out the walls of the ground floor, but it was big enough to stage a huge wedding. The catering staff would have to work out of tents hidden at the back of the property, and they'd have to hire luxurious mobile bathrooms.

It was going to require a lot of additional cash. Good thing that Micah and Jago, who were paying for Thadie's wedding, had lots of that particular commodity.

Ella walked over to where Micah and Samuel stood. Micah pulled her to his side and dropped a kiss on her temple. Ella loved his easy affection and she responded by winding her arm around his waist.

Samuel noticed their connection as his eyes went to where Micah's hand rested on her hip. Ella waited for him to wind down—he was saying something about some cricket tour—but, when it looked as if he had no intention of shutting up, Ella interrupted him.

'It has possibilities,' she told Micah. 'I'd need to come back, measure up properly and gather some more information before I can present it as a decent option to our interested party.'

'Who needs a venue? And for what?' Samuel asked, his eyes glinting with waspish curiosity.

Ella jumped in before Micah could answer. 'We're keeping the identity of my client a secret, Mr Dobson.'

If Dobson knew the wedding was for Thadie, he'd either use the information to cop an invitation or leak it to the press.

'Would you consider hiring out the house and the grounds for a weekend?' Ella asked him.

'For the right price. Obviously, it'll be an enormous upheaval, so I'd have to be adequately compensated.'

You mean you need the cash, Ella thought, mentally rolling her eyes.

If he'd had funds, he would've finished the renovation. How stupid did he think they were? But, okay, she'd play his game. 'Would you object to some minor touch-ups?'

'Like what?' Samuel demanded.

'Painting the veranda, some of the inside walls. Neutral colours, of course. If I can, I'll try to match the original colour as closely as possible.' *The way it was before your insensitive, cloddish renovations.* Ella managed a small smile. 'Will you think about it and, if you agree, let me know?'

He shrugged, looking sulky. 'As I said, it will be a massive inconvenience,' Samuel whined. Ella knew that as soon as they left, he'd research rental charges for weddings and would at least quadruple the the going rate.

Micah placed a hand on her back and steered her towards the front door. On the front steps, he shook Dobson's hand, told him to call as soon as possible, walked her to his Bentayga and opened the passenger door for her.

They were halfway down the driveway when Micah turned to her. 'Are you okay? You seemed a bit off in there.'

She debated whether to tell him, then decided that she would. She trusted Micah not to dismiss her feelings. 'Your friend gives me the creeps. He spent more time talking to my breasts than my face.'

God, she was so sick of shutting down, retreating

when she felt uncomfortable. She was tired of pulling into herself, mentally rolling into a tight ball and hiding in the corner when she felt even a little hot male interest. Yet Micah, whose eyes frequently blazed with desire, never once made her feel that way.

Micah hit the brake and the car came to an immediate stop. 'Did he say something to you when I stepped out to take that call? Did he try to grope you?'

Micah looked furious and she rushed to reassure him. 'No, nothing like that,' she answered him, lifting one shoulder. 'He was just creepy, that's all.'

Micah lifted her chin so that she had to look into his eyes. 'If you feel that way about anybody, ever, walk away. You don't have to experience that again, El.'

She appreciated the sentiment, but it wasn't a practical solution. As an event planner, she met all sorts of men all the time. Many—most—were decent, but there would always be one or two who'd try their luck, ask her out or try to cop a feel and laugh it off, claiming it was just a joke. She couldn't keep running away; she had to learn to live in the world as it was and not how she wanted it to be.

'Don't see him alone, okay?' After dropping an open-mouthed kiss on her lips, Micah pulled away. At the stop sign at the end of the road, he looked at her. 'I need to tell you something.'

The serious note in his voice caused every muscle in her body to contract. It was late Sunday afternoon, and the end of the weekend, and he was calling it quits. She felt as if she was standing on the edge of a chasm, about to fall.

'I received an email from my PI regarding his investigation into Neville Pillay.'

If he was about to break up with her, why was Micah mentioning him? And what did his PI have to do with it?

'I don't understand.' Ella managed to push her words up her throat and over her tongue.

'He's tracked down a significant number of women Pillay has harassed over the years, most of whom are prepared to make an official statement accusing him of sexual harassment and, in one case, attempted rape.'

Ella gripped the bridge of her nose. Okay, so he wasn't breaking up with her. Good news. Right, now she could concentrate on what he was telling her about Pillay.

'I'm sad to hear about all of those women but happy your PI has made so much progress.' She sent Micah a quick look. 'So what's next?'

Micah's smile was cold and hard. 'I'm going to leak the story to a journalist I trust. It'll be headline news in a few days. After doing her research, Kendall, the journalist, will, officially, call me for a comment. Jago and I will then release a statement saying that, on investigation, one of our employees was sexually accosted by Pillay and that we are terminating our association with him and his entertainment company.'

Ella was thankful that he would be exposed but she still had a question. 'Why couldn't you release a statement like that when I first told you about what he did?'

Micah didn't hesitate to answer her question. 'Because—sadly and wrongly—one woman's accusations, even with our support, don't have the same impact of a dozen or more accusations. He could've said that you led him on and that we were overreacting by firing him. This way, he has many, many questions to answer and there's a damn good chance he'll lose his career—definitely his reputation,' Micah explained. 'Naturally, we'll keep your name out of the papers.'

Ella nodded, glad that Pillay would never be in a position of power again. Strong men, as Micah had taught her, didn't need to wield their power like a burning sword. It was over and she could move on.

But to what? And where? Was emigrating still a reasonable option? How on earth was she going to live anywhere in the world without being able to see him, touch him, talk to him and love him? Because, judging by her reaction when she'd thought Micah was breaking up with her, she couldn't.

I'm prepared to let you hire my house for your client's wedding, I've emailed you a quote. We'll need to have a very boring discussion about the finer details—parking and bridal suites and space for the caterers and bar staff—and I'm sure Micah's time is too valuable to waste on things we can decide between us. I can see you at six this evening.

Ella, working from Hadleigh House, scowled down at the screen of her phone and tasted the sour panic at the back of her throat. Cathcart House was beautiful, historic and, after Anna de Palmer-Whyte and her team got hold of it, would be the perfect backdrop for Thadie's romantic wedding.

It was a flawless solution and she was the person who'd found it. The only problem—a huge one, in her view—was that Samuel Dobson wanted her to meet him alone at the huge, isolated house set in two acres of private grounds.

The price to rent the house as a wedding venue was steep but it was clear that Dobson wanted something a great deal more personal. Her.

Ella picked up her phone and sent a return message.

I am unavailable tonight. Could we meet in the morning?

Tonight suits me better. Or we could forget the idea.

Dammit, dammit, dammit, Ella thought as she typed a reply, telling him that she'd get back to him soon.

She didn't like Dobson. She really didn't want to meet him alone but she didn't know whether she was overreacting or not. She didn't know what to do.

She desperately wanted to talk to Micah about this, to get his down to earth, pragmatic point of view. He had a way of cutting through her emotion to reveal the heart of the problem, what was truth and what was perception. She knew she could show him her biggest fear, knowing he wouldn't mock or dismiss her.

She trusted him.

Ella placed her chin in her hand. She trusted him and she loved him. She loved that under the charming facade was a dented and damaged man, someone who

had his own scars and issues; that he was imperfect
but he kept showing up, trying to win at life. He was
honourable and honest and, once he pulled you under
his protection, you stayed there. He could've forgotten
about Brianna, accepted that bad things happened and
carried on with his life. But instead of doing that he'd
carried her with him and had tried to make the lives
of the people he loved better, easier. Micah took complete responsibility for his actions, determined not to
repeat past mistakes.

Taking on the responsibility of finding Thadie a
wedding venue was a perfect illustration of his sense of
responsibility. He didn't need to—he could've handed
the problem back to Thadie, Clyde and their wedding
planner—but, because in his mind it was his job to
smooth their paths, he'd taken on the work. Did the
rest of his family take advantage of that? Maybe. But
she also accepted that, once Micah decided to do something, wild horses couldn't stop him.

He was a strong, stubborn, sexy man, someone
she'd told herself she could not fall for, but she had.
She was so in love with him, and these were sen-
sations she'd never experienced before. Her feelings
weren't tempered by frustration and neither was she
wearing rose-coloured glasses. She knew Micah, she
loved him...

But Ella couldn't shake the feeling that the scales
of whatever they had were uneven, definitely tipped
in Micah's favour. And, no, she wasn't talking about
wealth or business influence—she couldn't compete
with him there. No, this was far more subtle than that.

Micah was completely self-confident, at ease with himself and his place in the world. He didn't second-guess himself or struggle with decision making and wasn't scared of people or situations. He knew exactly what he could offer the world…

Whereas she was still trying to figure out how to navigate her life.

She wanted to be his equal, to be strong, to claim her power and her confidence. And to do that she *had* to move past what had happened in the past.

Her mum had died because her dad hadn't believed her, but then why should he have automatically believed the word of a teenager? He was the one with the life experience and it had been a reasonable assumption that her mother would be fine after she slept off her midday drinking. He couldn't have been expected to believe in a teenager's gut instinct, a young woman with absolutely no medical experience. It was time to let her anger, hurt, and resentment go.

And she had to stop worrying so much about whether she was believed or not. Micah believed in her and, more importantly, she believed in herself. She could not carry on letting what had happened affect her self-worth. Micah had said to her, quite a few times now, that she was incredibly strong to have handled what she'd experienced on her own—both as a teenager and recently—and maybe it was time she believed that. It was definitely time to take back her power. She knew the truth, Micah knew the truth and that was all that mattered.

But…making a mental shift was one thing. How was she going to translate that into her daily life? If she stayed in South Africa, opened up her own business—and that scenario was looking more and more likely—and continued to see Micah, she couldn't expect him to be there every time she needed to meet a man for business. This meeting with Dobson was a good example of her dilemma. How would she be effective at her job if she didn't overcome her fear? How could she organise events if she couldn't meet with chefs, lighting guys, stage builders and two dozen other types of supplier without wanting to hide in a corner?

Pillay had taken that away from her. He'd made her scared to do her job but she was damned if she'd let him do that to her any more.

Micah had helped her come into her power and, for the first time in a long time, she felt confident in her ability to stand up for herself. Meeting Dobson alone would be the first test, the first steps on this new journey.

She knew she could handle herself, and him if necessary. The stakes were too great for her to fail.

But, because she wasn't one hundred per cent comfortable with Dobson, she'd ask Janie to come with her. She didn't need a bodyguard, but she wasn't foolish enough to go with no back-up at all.

She could do this; she *would* do this. Securing Dobson's agreement to stage Thadie's wedding at Cathcart House would be her present to Micah.

And, possibly more importantly, it would be a massive gift to herself.

Ella picked up her phone and made a call. 'Janie, what are you doing tonight around six? I need your help.'

CHAPTER ELEVEN

MICAH RUSHED INTO his office, uncharacteristically late. He dumped his leather briefcase on his desk, pulled out a couple of folders and grimaced. He had just a few hours to prep for an important meeting with a Swedish businesswoman who wanted to offload her small chain of English malls. Le Roux International owned a few properties in the UK, but this was a mega-money deal, and Erna Morganssen was reputed to be as quick as a whip and not above trying to take more than her piece of flesh.

But he'd caught Ella admiring his body in the mirror in the bathroom and that had led to some very creative fun on the bathroom floor. Thanks to indulging, he was now more than an hour behind schedule.

Worth it, though.

Micah heard the brief rap on his door and looked up to see his twin standing in his doorway, his face thunder-cloud dark. Oh, God, what now?

'I know you have bad news, Jay, I can see it on your face. But if no one has died, can it wait? I have an online meeting with Erna—'

'Have you seen the papers this morning?' Jago demanded, stepping into the office and shutting his office door behind him.

Micah sent him an irritated look. 'No. As I said, can this wait—?'

'Look online, twin,' Jago told him, nodding to his massive screen.

Right, Jago wasn't backing down. Micah sighed, sat down in his leather chair and booted up his computer. Jago loomed over his desk. Micah wished he could have one day without drama.

He pulled up his Internet browser and raised one eyebrow at his brother, silently asking where to go.

Jago walked to stand beside him, pulled Micah's wireless keyboard to him and rapidly typed. Micah caught the search results—something to do with Thadie—before Jago clicked on one of the more reputable entertainment sites, where the headline flashed...

Trouble in Paradise?

Yesterday we learned that Thadie Le Roux, South Africa's favourite heiress, asked her future in-law to step down as one of her bridesmaids. It's often been noted that Thadie and her fiancé's stepsister aren't close, but it seems like their relationship is a lot more fraught than any of us suspected.

We've also noticed that it's been a while since we've seen Thadie and Clyde out socialising together, as they used to do. Thadie attended two

charity events solo recently, and did not accom-
pany Clyde to the prestigious Protea & Passion
Sports Awards, a glittering event to honour our
country's best sportsmen and women.
*   Have they drifted apart?*

Micah leaned back in his chair and rubbed his
thumb and fingers along his forehead before looking
at his twin. He gestured to the screen. 'Do they know
about the wedding venue snafu?'

Jago leaned against his desk, his eyes steel-hard.
'No. And I don't understand why not. I mean, I
would've thought that news would've made it to the
press before Thadie firing Alta as a bridesmaid. Far
more people knew about the wedding venue being cancelled than Thadie's unhappiness with Alta.' He pushed
his hand through his hair. 'As a result of this, there's
been a spike in people trolling Thadie on social media.'

Micah cursed. He loved his sister, but he couldn't
deny that he'd be happy when this wedding was behind
them. But then that would mean Ella would be gone,
living ten thousand miles away. The thought was in-
comprehensible.

'I'll call Thadie when I have a moment,' Micah told
Jago, frowning when he heard the discreet buzz of his
intercom system: his PA needed to talk to him. On arriving at his office, he'd told her he didn't want to be
disturbed. Jago was the one person exempt from that
directive.

'Am I ever going to get to work today?' he grumbled, before issuing a voice instruction to turn the intercom system on.

'There's a Mrs Pearson to see you, sir. She doesn't have an appointment.'

Micah closed his eyes, irritated. He'd specifically told her that he wasn't to be disturbed, that he needed a solid block of four hours to concentrate. She could only interrupt him if the building was on fire or if there was an arterial blood spray...

Hold on—had she said Mrs Pearson? As in, Brianna's mother? Micah looked at Jago and frowned. 'Sorry, *who*?'

'Mrs Pearson. She says she knew you as a boy.'

Micah looked at Jago and, when he saw the astonishment on his twin's face, he knew he wasn't hallucinating. *Okay, well...* Micah ran his suddenly damp hands down his thighs and rubbed his face, the side of his jaw. What did she want? Why was she here? Was Brianna dead? No, if that had happened she wouldn't have come to his offices or he would've heard the news via Liyana.

The only way to know what she wanted was to let her in but Micah didn't want to. He'd only seen Kate Pearson twice since the accident, and both of those meetings had happened shortly before Bri had been moved from the local hospital into a long-term care facility. Kate and Phil had refused to see him after that, wouldn't take his calls or respond to his emails. They had severed their relationship with his father and stepmother as well.

'Micah?'

'Yes, I'm coming,' he replied.

'Do you want me to stay?' Jago asked him, looking concerned.

Micah sent his brother a grateful look. 'No, I'll be fine.'

Jago left the room and closed the door behind him. Micah cleared his throat, took a sip from the water bottle on his desk and hauled in a deep breath. Heart thumping, he walked to the door, wishing he didn't feel as if he was eighteen again, wretched, remorseful and so damn guilty.

He wrenched his door open and there she stood, an aged version of Brianna, the young girl he'd once laughed with and loved in his way, as much as a wild, rebellious teenage boy could.

Micah didn't bother trying to shake her hand or even offer a smile. He knew that neither would be welcome. He simply inclined his head and waited until she had stepped into the office before hauling in more air—why was it suddenly so thin?—and following her inside.

He closed the door and gestured her to the couch where the seating was more comfortable. Kate sat down and linked her hands together. 'I suppose you want to know why I'm here...'

Well, yes. Obviously.

'I heard that Bri has a respiratory infection, that she's very ill. How is she?'

Kate released a long breath. 'She's struggling. She hasn't responded to the antibiotics.'

'I'm sorry to hear that, Kate.' He was so sorry about so much, had been for so long.

Kate's eyes—so blue, just like Brianna's—collided with his. 'Should I remove her feeding tube?'

What? Where had that come from?

Kate placed her elbows on her knees and clasped her head in her hands. 'I'm so tired, Micah. So tired of seeing her like that.'

Of course she was, that was understandable. What mother wanted to watch her child—a daughter who should've had a career, been a wife, a mum—lie in a bed, unresponsive? He couldn't, genuinely, think of anything worse.

But...

'I'm not sure what you want from me, Kate,' Micah said, trying to be as gentle as possible. Yes, this woman had caused him grief, but his was nothing to what she'd been through.

Kate sprang to her feet, walked over to his massive window and placed her hands on the glass. 'I need you to help me make a decision, Micah.'

Man, the blows didn't stop coming. Micah followed her over to the window and stood next to her, watching the matchbook-sized cars far below him. He knew what she meant, but selfishly he didn't want to be a part of this conversation. It was too hard, too monumental...

They were talking about someone's life, Bri's life, for God's sake!

'Phil refused to even consider the idea of letting her go and I've resisted thinking about it. But seeing her struggling to breathe is too much. And if she recovers, it'll just be another few months, maybe a year or two, before it happens again.'

'But why ask me, Kate? You hate me.'

Kate turned sad, empty eyes on him. 'I did, for a long time. But Bri adored you. From the time you met as toddlers, she only had eyes for you. She once told me that you knew her better than anyone, and vice versa.'

That had been true, up until Ella had arrived in his life. But, unlike Brianna, Ella didn't see him through rose-tinted glasses, she saw his flaws and contradictions, but seemed to like him anyway.

He didn't *like* her...he was crazily, stunningly, top-to-toe in love with her. He couldn't imagine his life without her in it and didn't know how he was going to cope if she left the country. He had four days until she officially left his employ. He hoped to have things sorted by then—her sharing his bed, permanently in his life.

But that was for later. He needed to concentrate on Kate right now.

'What would she want me to do, Micah?' Kate whispered.

Oh, God, he knew the answer to that, could hear Bri's lilting voice in his ear. *Tell her to let me go, Micah.*

'I don't want her to die, Kate,' he said, his voice croaky with emotion. 'But I hate the idea of her being kept alive, her condition never changing.'

'But what if she's in there somewhere?' Kate laid a hand on her heart. 'What if she comes back? People have, you know.'

Yes, he did, but Bri wouldn't.

He'd had a very detailed, scientific talk with one of

the world's best neurologists and he'd been told that, the longer she remained unresponsive, the less likely she'd ever recover.

Tell her to let me go, Micah. Set us all free.

He'd need the courage to say what he knew he ought to, what he knew Brianna would want, more courage than he'd ever needed before. Because, at the end of the day, there was a bit of a 'playing God' element to this. But hadn't they been playing God by keeping her alive with the feeding tube? He clenched his fist, not knowing what to say, how to frame his words.

Knowing that if he thought about this any more, if he allowed himself any more time, he'd lose his courage, so he gently placed his hands on Kate's shoulders. 'I'm not telling you what to do, Kate. I can't. But I know that Brianna would not like to live like this; in fact, she'd hate it. But the decision will always be yours. You've got to do what you can live with and, no matter what your decision is, I will always support you.'

Kate rested her forehead on his chest, breathing heavily. 'I've hated you for so long, Micah.'

'I know,' he whispered. He'd hated himself as well, but he was done with that now. He wasn't solely to blame for the tragedy that had beset Bri. She'd chosen to follow him, to get behind the wheel of her car.

It was Ella who'd made him believe in himself and in his life. Somehow, that gorgeous, straight-talking, completely wonderful woman had cracked the door on his dark inner world and let in some light. Then more. Solidly black things were now grey, rising to opaque.

Yes, he'd made mistakes—he shouldn't have stormed out and gone down to that bar in the first place—but Bri had made mistakes too. She'd also acted impulsively, stupidly.

So had Kate, Phil, Theo and Liyana. And, like him, they all had to live with the consequences of their actions.

Kate pulled back from him and pulled her fingertips under her eyes, collecting the few tears that had gathered there. She touched her neck, her eyes wary. 'I'm tired of fighting, hating, feeling sad and resentful.'

He understood that more than she knew. 'So am I, Kate.'

She swallowed and nodded. 'I'm not sure what I'm going to do. I'm not making any promises but…do you want me to let you know if I decide to…?'

He understood her reluctance to spell it out. It was too big for words. 'Yes, please.'

Kate nodded once, abruptly, and swiftly walked over to the couch, where she picked up her bag and pulled it over her shoulder. She gestured to the door. 'I'm going to go now.'

Staying where he was, Micah nodded. She had his entire sympathy—he couldn't imagine having to make such a hard decision on his own, and his heart bled for her. He felt exhausted and emotional but also relieved; progress had been made today.

He jammed his hands into the pockets of his suit. 'Kate?'

She turned to look at him. 'If you ever need to talk

again, to talk to someone who loved her and knew her, you can always talk to me. I was young and stupid, but I loved her.'

Her smile was small but there. 'Thank you, Micah.'

She walked out of his office and closed the door behind her. Micah, feeling battered, slid down the glass wall to sit on the carpet, his back to the window. He dropped his head and closed his eyes, fighting tears. Losing Brianna had hurt—it still hurt—but he didn't love her a fraction as much as he loved Ella.

How would he cope if he lost her? He wouldn't. He'd crawl into himself, shrivel up and die. Not to be dramatic, but he didn't want to live in a world that didn't have Ella in it.

What if something happened to her? What if he lost her, what if she left him? What if he was reading their relationship wrong and she still intended to get onto that London-bound plane next week?

What the hell had he been thinking, allowing her to get so close, to slide into his heart?

And why did he think that things were different with her, that he could have a normal life, that he even deserved to be happy? Kate was thinking about letting her child die and he'd been consumed by thoughts of Ella—occasionally even allowing himself to think about having her as his wife, living with her at Hadleigh House, being a husband and a father.

What the hell was wrong with him?

Micah didn't make his meeting with the Swedish businesswoman. Or any other meeting that day.

* * *

It was much later that evening when Ella stepped out
of the lift on the top floor of Le Roux International and
looked around the empty reception area, wondering
where the twins' second-shift PA was— they worked
insane hours and needed after-hours help. She looked
at the opaque glass walls of Micah's office, frustrated
that she couldn't see inside. She didn't want to barge
in on Micah if he was in a meeting, but she'd just come
from seeing Dobson and she wanted to share her news.

Pulling her phone out of her bag, she banged out a
quick message to Micah, asking what he was doing.
His reply was brief.

At my desk, working.

Great, it sounded as if he was alone. Walking across
the spacious area, she knocked on his office door and
pushed her way in. Micah sat behind his desk, his head
in his hands and his shoulders hunched. He jerked up
abruptly but his face was sheet-white and his eyes red
with fatigue...

It had to be fatigue because he couldn't possibly
have been crying, could he? 'What are you doing here?'
he demanded. His happy-to-see-you smile was absent.

She dropped her bag onto the seat of the closest
chair. 'I need to run something by you. Are you okay?'

Every hint of emotion drained from his eyes and
face as he sat back and, very deliberately, placed his
ankle on his knee. He looked past her to his door.

'Since when do you barge into my private office without my permission?'

Ella glanced back at the door, winced and shrugged. 'Your PA wasn't at her desk.' She pushed away her embarrassment at being scolded like a junior employee. She had more important things to discuss right now.

'Sorry, I know you have a lot on your plate, but I need to talk to you.'

'Could it not wait until I had time to talk to *you*?'

Wow, he was in a snit. She'd never seen him so cold, so irritated. Well, he'd soon get over it when she told him her news.

She'd start with the good news first. 'I think it's a go for Cathcart House.'

His expression didn't change. 'What are you talking about, Ella?'

'I went to see Samuel Dobson, and he and I hammered out an agreement in principle. I've arranged for Thadie and Anna to meet me there tomorrow morning and, if you can make it, I'd love you to be there too.'

Micah stood up slowly and placed his hands on his desk, his expression thunderous. 'You went to see him? On your own?'

Ella's temper started to heat. 'I was doing my job, Micah. The job you hired me to do.'

'I ordered you not to go there!' Micah shouted.

He'd ordered her? *What?* When they'd discussed Samuel, he'd been talking as her lover, not her boss.

'I cannot believe that you would be so stupid, after everything you've been through, to meet him on your own. What if he did something to you, what if he tried something?' Micah yelled, every syllable rising in volume. He caught something on her face and his expression— -summer-thunderstorm-intense—darkened. 'What did he do? He did something, didn't he?'

'He asked me out,' Ella reluctantly admitted. 'I said no.'

'What else?'

Samuel had been pretty persistent, telling her that she needn't be loyal to Micah, because he'd never been loyal to a woman in his life. Micah didn't make commitments, he said, and didn't believe in monogamy. After steering the conversation back to business three times after the fourth time Dobson had raised the subject, she lost it and told him to shut the hell up. She'd then gone on to give him a loud and exhaustive lecture on consent and persistence. She'd also made it clear that she wasn't a toy to be fought over.

Janie, who had waited in the car and listened in via the call Ella had started before going inside, had told her that it was a masterful put-down. And, kudos to her, Janie continued, that she'd still managed to seal the deal to hire Cathcart House. Ella was convinced it was mainly down to the fact that Dobson was hurting for money and not because he was contrite.

She didn't want to fight with Micah so she pulled the conversation back to business. 'So, do you think you can meet us tomorrow?'

'I'm not done talking about the fact that you went there alone!' Micah snapped. Right, he was determined to pick a fight with her. Why?

'Well, I am!'

'After what you went through, why would you take that chance?' He walked around the desk and cupped her face in his hands, looking at her intently. His face softened and his thumbs skated over her cheekbones. 'Are you okay? You know, mentally? Did it bring up any bad memories? Do you want to talk about it?'

'Micah, I'm *fine*.'

They turned at a sharp rap on the door and Ella spun round to see Jago standing in the doorway. He sent Ella a distracted smile and focused on his twin. 'Sorry, I only just managed to wrap up my meetings now. Micah, are you okay? What did Kate Pearson want? Is Brianna…?'

Micah shook his head. 'No, she's alive.' Micah kept his eyes on Jago, waves of emotion rolling through his eyes. 'I was coming to see you, to talk it out with you, but then Ella arrived unexpectedly. I'll be with you in five, ten minutes.'

So, she wasn't welcome to stay. And it was obvious he had no intention of telling her about his out-of-the-blue conversation with Brianna's mother. It was also obvious that Kate's visit had blown up Micah's day, but he wanted to talk to his twin, not to her.

When his world fell apart, she wasn't the person to whom he could turn.

Jago left and Ella gripped the back of the nearest chair, using it to help support her wobbly legs and keep her body upright. Micah wanted her physically, and might even enjoy her company, but she wasn't good enough or important enough to help him deal with the big things, the important things.

Micah looked back at her. 'Sorry about that. Are you sure you're okay? What can I do for you, Fl? What do you need? And, sorry, I still don't understand why you went over there without me!'

Why was he trying to fix something that wasn't broken? Ella stepped away from the chair, frowning. What was going on here? Ella touched her top lip with the tip of her tongue. Was he angry at her for going to Dobson alone, or mad because she hadn't allowed him the chance to play the Great Protector? Because that was what Micah did, he protected and fixed, rearranged his world to patch people and situations back together. Making things right was what he did, who he was...

He couldn't fix Brianna but he could fix her. Was she just another one of his projects?

She thought that she just might be. And when he deemed her to be fixed, having knocked out her dings and dents, he'd send her back out into the world.

But that wasn't what she wanted. She wanted him to love her with her dings and dents, scratches and knocks. She wanted to be able to be exactly who she was at every minute of the day. She might feel confident, then scared, unsure and then powerful, and she wanted him to ride those waves with her, let her fly down them when she was feeling assured and to catch her when the wave swept her off her feet.

But Micah only wanted smooth waters or to control the tides.

And it was obvious to Ella that when the storms built up in his life he wasn't going to turn to her for help, comfort or advice.

Ella felt tears burning the back of her eyes. 'I can't be who you need me to be, Micah.'

'What the hell do you mean by that?'

'Because of what happened to Brianna, you need to be the one in control of the situation, looking around to see who you can help, who you can fix. Because you can't fix her.' Ella bit down hard on her bottom lip, tasting blood.

'I am not talking about Brianna. I am talking about the fact that you went to see Dobson on your own,' Micah said, biting out the words.

'I'm not a child, Micah! And, for your information, Janie sat in the car while I met with him and my phone was connected to hers the whole time. I made a mistake with Pillay, but I am not stupid!'

'I never said that you were!'

'No, but you think I'm weak, and that's part of your attraction to me.' She saw something flash in his eyes, an acknowledgement that her words had hit the target. Oh, God, it hurt. It hurt knowing that his attraction was wrapped up in him perceiving her to be weaker than him, with his need to protect and fix. Ella knew that she had a choice to make, and she had to do it right now.

She could either let Micah guard her mentally and physically, allow him the opportunity to feed his need to keep protecting her. She'd have to keep swallowing down her frustration, but she'd be with him. But in time he'd get bored of doing that and, in a week, month or year, he'd break up with her.

Her other option was for her to claim her power, insist that he treat her as an emotional and mental equal, that he see her as a strong and competent woman. If she did that, she knew he'd break up with her straight away. She could either be a half-version of herself with Micah or a full version of herself without him.

It was a hell of a choice.

But, in the end, she needed to live in truth, her truth. She needed to look after herself first because nobody else would. Ella straightened and pushed her hands into her hair.

'I can't remain broken so that you can feel better, Micah. I can't make myself less because you need a problem to fix, someone to protect. I can only be me, and I want to be fully me—strong, confident, powerful. I want to be in a healthy relationship, a place where I can be strong for you, where you can be the same for me. I want to feel free to make mistakes, to do my own thing, for you to be proud of me when I succeed, to be my soft place to fall when I mess up. I want to do the same thing for you but, judging by the fact that you will talk to your brother but not to me, I know that's never going to happen. I don't want you to try and fix me, Micah, because I am *not* broken!'

Ella bent down, picked up her bag and slung it over her shoulder. She needed to leave, to walk out of his building and his life before she fell apart. 'I really think Cathcart House is perfect for Thadie; I suggest you give it serious attention. And just pay me the quarter-million pounds, the original amount we decided on. I don't want any more.'

Micah looked both shocked and confused. 'Ella, what the hell? Where are you going?'

She looked around. 'Right now, I am going home to my empty flat. And then I'm booking a flight to London. Then I'm going to start a new life...*again*. I thought I wanted to start one with you, but you want me to be someone I'm not prepared to be any more, Micah.'

She reached the door, placed her hand on the frame and turned round to look at him. Six-foot-three of pure frustration, anger and confusion. 'Oh, and I'm also going to contact that reporter, Kendall, and tell her that I was accosted by Neville Pillay. I refuse to hide any more, and I want to control the narrative of *my* story. And, maybe if I come forward, it'll give other women the courage to step out of the darkness and tell their stories.'

She loved him and she was walking away from him. But she had to; this was the right thing to do. For her. 'Bye, Micah.'

Refusing to cry, Ella pushed her shoulders back and left. In the empty lift, she rested her forehead against the mirrored panel and closed her eyes, feeling her heart starting to rip and then crumble.

CHAPTER TWELVE

MICAH STILL COULDN'T get Ella's stricken face out of his mind.

Leaning back in his chair, he threw down his expensive ballpoint pen— a gift from Thadie two Christmases ago—and scowled at the contract he'd been making notes on. Or not making notes on, since he was still on page two, which comprised nothing more than definitions.

There was no point in trying to work. His brain— and his heart—simply wouldn't cooperate. All they wanted to do was replay yesterday's catastrophic events.

Micah freely admitted that Kate's visit earlier in the day had rocked him. He couldn't stop thinking about their discussion, and the knowledge that he'd encouraged her to end Brianna's suffering ate at him. Had he said the right thing? Did he even have any right to an opinion? They were talking about ending someone's *life*! Had he been too glib, too quick to rush to judgement? Should he have given it some more thought?

But he knew, with every part of him, that Brianna would have hated living in a hospital bed.

On arriving at work after a sleepless night—he'd missed having Ella in his house and his bed—he'd told his PA he'd fire her if she put a call through or let anyone into his office, and he'd tried to focus on work. But he'd made little progress as his thoughts kept bouncing between his conversations with Kate and Ella.

He remembered Ella's initial reaction to hearing about Bri. Her take on the situation had been considered and wise and had left him feeling that he could have a full life, allow himself to be happy, fall in love...

Fall in love? He'd done that already. Somewhere, some time in the past two and a half weeks, he'd fallen in love with Ella and wanted her in his life on a permanent basis. He wanted her living with him in Hadleigh House, waking up with him, being beside him when he reached for her in the night. He wanted to have children with her, cousins for Thadie's twins.

Because he'd really opened up to her, more than he ever had to anyone—even Jago—she was now his closest confidante. She knew his quirks and his flaws, his secrets and his ambitions, who he was at the core of his soul. But he'd spectacularly sabotaged his life yesterday.

Ella had accused him of wanting to fix the world because he couldn't fix Bri—true enough—but he only wanted to fix *his* section of it. He'd spent twenty years trying to make up for what had happened to Bri and, because he couldn't fix her, he did everything he could to help out his siblings, working hard so as not to disappoint them. Or Jabu.

But Jago and Thadie were smart, healthy and wealthy

individuals and they didn't need his input or his help. They were fully able to make their own decisions and live with the consequences.

As Ella had said, he was the family fixer, but he was done with that.

But what she'd got very wrong was this idea that he thought she was broken.

God, how could she think that? Ella was the most together, the strongest, woman he'd ever met. She'd stated that she wanted to be powerful and confident but she didn't realise that she already was. She'd been emotionally knocked around—more than once—but she'd got up, dusted herself down and kept fighting. When her life had flipped upside down, she'd wrestled with the world until she'd been able to make a plan, start again. She'd never stopped fighting and she'd done it alone.

That was what amazed him the most: Ella had gone through so much and she'd done it without parents, siblings or a support structure. He was in awe of her strength and capability. The last thing she was broken.

And, yes, he was over-protective of her—admittedly, he'd overreacted about her going to Cathcart House alone. But it was because he wanted her to know that she had someone on her side, someone who was prepared to go to war for her. He'd been trying to show her that she didn't have to be alone, that he'd always protect and cherish her, that he wanted to be the one she turned to when her life felt off-kilter.

Micah saw Jago walk past his open office door and frowned, recalling that Ella had said something about

Jago last night. Amid everything else she'd lobbed at his head, he'd forgotten that detail. What had she said?

Something about Brianna…that when his life fell apart, he turned to Jago and not to her.

He did, that was true. He and Jago had shared a womb, and had been each other's comfort and strength during their volatile childhood. His brother was his best friend and Jago had known Brianna—she'd been a part of both their childhoods—so it was natural for Micah to want to talk to Jago about Kate's visit, about Brianna…

Confiding in Jago was also a habit.

The woman he loved and trusted, whose opinion he respected, had stood in front of him and, instead of talking to her about his awful day, he'd gone into 'fix it' mode to make him feel that he had control of something. Nothing could ever happen to Ella, so his protective instinct had risen and taken over.

And, when he'd seen Jago, he said that he'd explain Kate's visit to him. He'd made it sound as if he'd had no intention of talking to Ella. But he had—he'd wanted to tell her everything.

Still did.

Micah recalled the pain in her eyes and gripped the bridge of his nose. He'd hurt her, something he'd promised himself he'd never do—not her or any other woman. God, he… *He'd messed up.*

His private mobile phone rang and he snatched it up. 'Ella? Where are you?'

'Sorry, it's just me,' Thadie replied. 'You know, your

sister? The one who's entertaining the country with her wedding disaster woes?'

Look, he loved Thadie, but on this occasion he needed to put Ella first. 'Sorry, Thads, I know you're going through hell, but I need to find Ella...'

Thadie was silent for a couple of beats. 'I was phoning *you* to find her. We were supposed to meet her at Cathcart House this morning—she sent me a message last night—but she's not here. She did email us a detailed proposal of why she thinks the house will work for the wedding, though—and, Micah, it's fabulous. It's everything I want! Anna is so impressed with Ella, she wants to know if she'll consult on other weddings, but I can't reach her.'

Ella had done as he'd asked—found him a venue and made his sister incredibly happy. God, he loved her.

'Why can't *you* get hold of Ella, Micah?' Thadie demanded. 'What did you do?'

'I messed up,' Micah confessed, a cold hand squeezing his heart.

'Well, Anna and I need her help with this wedding and you, brother, need her in your life. She makes you happy, Micah—and, God, you need some happy!'

He'd already come to that conclusion. 'I do,' he agreed.

'Then why the hell aren't you trying to get her back?'

Good question, Micah thought. Sitting behind his desk doing nothing wouldn't make her stroll back into his life. She was the air he breathed, the reason his sun rose, the beat of his heart...all those clichés that were clichés because they were so damned powerful and true.

She was what he needed. Now, later, tomorrow, sixty years from now.

His world would, if she left him, stop turning. It was that simple and that dramatic.

He was good at fixing things but this would be the biggest repair job of his life. He hoped he was up to it.

Ella sat cross-legged on her couch, her laptop resting on her thighs, listlessly searching for a flight to London. She'd been crying off and on for nearly twenty-four hours and didn't think she'd stop any time soon. She'd run out of tissues and had moved on to toilet paper to mop her eyes and blow her nose, and she was down to her last roll.

But the thought of leaving her flat was too much to contemplate, so when she ran out of loo roll she'd move onto kitchen towel. Anything was better than leaving her flat…

Another thing she couldn't do was to make a booking for her flight. Her credit card sat on the cushion next to her, but she couldn't choose a date or a time… she wasn't able to punch in the numbers, make the commitment.

She didn't want to go. She didn't want to leave Johannesburg…she didn't want to leave Micah. She wanted a life with him, to be his lover and his partner, to navigate life with him. But she needed to be an equal partner, able to give as well as receive. And, while she didn't want to come between him and his twin, she wanted to be the person he turned to first, his best friend and confidante. She also wanted them to be a team, facing the world together, a couple with equal stakes in the relationship.

Micah could pretend that they were not in a relationship, but from the moment they admitted their attraction they'd started the slide down that particular hill. They were not having a fling, an affair, or a three-week stand. He might not be in love with her but she did mean something—possibly quite a lot—to him. But, judging by his silence—she hadn't heard from him since she'd left his office yesterday—she didn't mean enough.

And, if she couldn't have everything, she'd rather walk away. She couldn't force him to be with her. Love that was coerced was just another strategy in the game of power and control. She was done with that nonsense.

Gathering her courage, Ella chose a flight for early the next week and punched in her credit card details. A confirmation number flashed up on her screen and she closed her eyes, tears coursing down her cheeks.

It was done. She was going to the UK where, yet again, she'd have to start over. Alone.

She should be used to it by now.

Ella closed her laptop, looked at the scads of crumpled tissue on her couch and floor and told herself to clean up, to pick herself up. But she didn't have the energy to do anything right now. She just wanted to sit here and mourn what could've been.

Grieve for the life she could envision but couldn't have.

* * *

Micah sat on the bench under his favourite oak tree, his head tipped back to look at the moonlight filtering through the leaves of the trees. It was a perfectly still night, hot and warm, and he couldn't hear a frog or a cricket. It was as if the world was holding its breath…

He certainly was.

He glanced at his watch and saw that it was nearly midnight. His shoulders slumped, and he checked his phone again, but it remained stubbornly silent. After running around all day, making offers and signing documents, he'd texted Ella around ten, asking if she could do him one last thing and meet him at Hadleigh House.

She'd oh-so-formally replied that she'd be there in an hour. He had Jabu waiting to meet her and bring her to him, but so far he'd heard nothing from either his butler or the love of his life. She wasn't coming; he'd lost her. His gamble hadn't paid off.

Micah cursed and bent over, holding his head in his hand. What the hell was he supposed to do now?

'It's late, Micah. I can't think why you've asked me to come here at this time of night.'

His head shot up. He looked down the path and there she was, moonlight touching her dark hair. He took in the details, drinking her in. She wore another of her simple sundresses and beaded flip-flops. Her hair was pulled back in a low ponytail but her face was still shadowed.

He needed to see her eyes, to look into her beautiful face. He needed to do that now and…when he was eighty, ninety…hers was the first and last face he'd want to see.

Micah picked up the tablet that lay on the bench next to him, hit a tab and the garden lit up, transforming into a wonderland of light and shadow that was fantastically romantic. Ella looked around and nodded. 'Your house is even prettier at night than it is in the day. But I still don't know why I'm here.'

How to tell her? Micah picked an opening line, considered it and discarded it. Frankly, words were currently impossible, so he patted the bench beside him. She reached him, sat down and crossed one luscious leg over the other, tipping her head back to look up into the branches of the tree. 'Switch off the lights, Micah.'

He killed the lights and immediately heard the sound of a bullfrog croaking, the buzz of a mosquito, the call of a nightjar. Ella's perfume, the aroma light and fresh, hit his nose and his soul settled. She was here, where she was meant to be.

He had to say something so he settled on the easy stuff. 'I transferred the money to your account today.'

'Thank you.' Judging by her still cool tone, he knew that she'd assumed he'd paid her just two hundred and fifty thousand. She'd get a shock when she saw that her account had been credited with an additional five hundred thousand. The amount didn't matter, though; he'd give her *everything* if he could.

'And Thadie and Anna love your ideas for the wedding.'

'So Thadie is going to have her wedding at Cathcart House?' Ella asked him, but her voice still didn't hold much excitement.

'She is. She's been trying to call you.'

Ella shrugged. 'I turned my mobile off. I didn't want to talk to anybody.'

'I think you should talk to her because Thadie wants to know whether she can give your number to Anna; apparently she's looking for a consultant, someone with flair and innovation. Someone who could, possibly, take over her business some day.'

He was gratified by the shock on her face, the hint of delight he saw in her eyes. But it quickly faded and he cursed himself for hurting her so badly that she couldn't take pleasure in a well-deserved opportunity.

'I'm going to the UK, Micah, I booked my ticket.'

He couldn't bear it. 'Don't go.' He choked out the words.

'Why should I stay?'

He hauled in a deep breath. 'Don't go because I messed up, El.'

'I'm going because you can't give me what I need.' Ella leaned forward, her forearms resting on her thighs.

'I don't think you are broken, Ella, and I don't consider you someone who needs to be fixed. I'm in awe of who you are, what you've achieved, how you've handled being battered by life. Life might've put you through the wringer lately, but you are far stronger than you give yourself credit for. Far braver, too.'

'I'm not brave,' Ella scoffed.

How could she believe that? 'Seeing Dobson on your own was brave. Agreeing to talk to that reporter about what Pillay did to you is incredibly courageous, Ella. So many women are going to take inspiration from your story and find their courage to come forward about him and other men. I am in awe of you,' Micah told her, his emotions evident in his voice.

'Yesterday was a very bad day, Ella, but you're right. I should've spoken to you as soon as you walked in the door instead of doing what I normally do—going into fix-and-control-the-world mode. I hurt you by telling Jago that I'd talk to him about what had happened, and made you feel like I wouldn't come to you with the important things… I'm sorry about that.'

She turned her head to look at him, concern in her eyes. 'Can you tell me now?'

He nodded. 'I'd like to.' He placed a hand on her back, needing to touch her. She didn't pull away and that tiny gesture gave him hope. 'Kate came to see me.'

'Brianna's mum?'

He nodded. 'She's thinking about letting Bri go, and she wanted my opinion on what Bri would want.'

Ella laid her hand on her heart. 'Oh, Micah, that must've been such a hard conversation.'

He nodded. 'It rocked me—totally derailed me, in fact—and I spent the rest of the day second-guessing myself because I told her that Brianna would hate her situation. When you walked in, I was feeling sad and miserable and lousy. I redirected my anger at not being able to do anything onto you. Also, I just felt this overwhelming urge to protect you, to not have anything happen to you, and the thought of you being alone in a situation that could've gone wrong overwhelmed me. I'm sorry I overreacted.'

She nodded. 'Going to see Dobson alone wasn't easy for me to do, I admit that. I did take precautions, but I think I'd like to get a taser, learn some self-defence. If I know I can defend myself, that would make me feel less stressed about being on my own with strange men.'

And he would feel better about it too. He'd offer to teach her Krav Maga but he knew that they'd be distracted as soon as they put their hands on each other. 'I know an instructor who could teach you enough to feel confident about your ability to handle yourself. That's if you stay here…with me.'

He gestured to his house, the one he knew and loved, but not as much as he loved her. 'Stay with me, El—here at Hadleigh House. Or, if you didn't see yourself sharing the grounds with Jago and Dodi—'

'Jago and Dodi? Thadie's best friend and the owner of the bridal salon?'

Yeah, that isn't important right now! 'We can talk about my brother and his love life later.' Micah growled, frustrated. 'Can I buy you a house?' he asked suddenly.

She looked confused. 'A house? What house? What are you talking about?'

'The why is easy, because I'm comprehensively in love with you. For ever. I'm talking about Cathcart House. And, in the interest of full disclosure, I've already bought it.'

Ella looked as if she was battling to keep up. 'You bought it from Dobson?'

He shook his head. 'He's not the owner, he just manages it for them. He doesn't even live on the property any more. The consortium I mentioned the first day we spoke about the house? They own it and are happy to offload it.'

She rubbed the back of her neck, confusion on her face. 'You are ten steps ahead of me, Micah. Why would I want it?'

'You think I don't notice how you react to things but I do. I notice everything about you.' And he always would. 'I saw your face as you walked around that house the first time you saw it; you fell in love with it. I could see your wheels churning, thinking about how you would fix this, do that. I thought you might want to run your business from there, use it to stage events, weddings and parties and ladies' lunches...'

Since she wasn't jumping up and down with joy, he shrugged. 'Or, if you want to, we can convert it back to a home and live there.'

She placed her hands on her cheeks, her eyes wide. 'Micah, God, *stop*! Give me a chance to catch up, my mind is spinning!'

Taking a deep breath, she held up her hand, which he took, kissing her palm. Desire flashed in her eyes and her hand trembled. He loved the way he affected her, but it was a fraction of how much she affected him.

'We'll come back to houses and my career in a minute. Let's go back a couple of steps. Did you mean it? What you said about loving me?'

Why did she look so shocked? Wasn't it written all over his face? 'El, sweetheart, you...you are the switch that flipped light onto my life again. Up until I looked up and saw you standing there, my life was muted. The only way I can describe it is that it was like one of those old-fashioned sepia photographs, the ones that only show shades of brown.'

He gently dragged his thumb along her jaw. 'You injected colour, conversation, life and laughter and great, emotional sex into my world, and I can't live without you. I don't *want* to live without you.'

Yes, it had happened quickly, but it wasn't any less powerful, as he told her. 'You might need some time to catch up but the fact that you are here with me gives me hope that you might, some time soon, feel the same way.'

She moved closer, close enough to slide her lips across his in a heart-resuscitating kiss. 'I don't need time. I love you too, Micah. So much.'

'Does that mean you will stay?'

Ella's fingertips drifted over his jaw. 'I'll stay because you are my person, Micah. Because you make me feel strong and capable and powerful—but, best of all, loved.'

He'd heard the expression about having a heart so full it felt as if it would burst, but Micah had never once thought he'd experience it himself until now, when his heart was so very close to doing exactly that. Micah swallowed, then swallowed again, unable to believe his luck. Or pull his eyes off her lovely face. The face he was going to be looking at for the rest of his life.

Then Ella scrunched up her face, her nose wrinkling. 'I need to call Anna, think about your crazy house offer, move the rest of my stuff into your place and cancel my ticket. Damn, I'm going to lose so much money when I do that.'

Micah laughed, enchanted by her making a list in the middle of the declarations of love. And he loved the fact that, despite offering to buy her a house that cost upwards of twenty million, she still cared about saving money. 'You can sell your bed and your couch. Maybe you'll get enough to cover your loss,' he teased, thinking of her fat-with-cash bank account which she'd obviously forgotten about.

'I mean, it's not like your future husband is rich and can afford to spoil you or anything like that,' he added, his voice cracking with emotion.

She laid her open palm on the side of his face and raised her eyebrows. 'My future husband?' she asked, her mouth dropping open. 'Are you proposing, Micah?'

'I am.' He turned his face to kiss her palm. 'I want to be your husband, lover, house mate, the father of the kids we're going to have...'

She mocked-glared at him. 'Only one at a time, Le Roux! I couldn't cope with twins.'

He pulled her onto his lap and kissed her laughing mouth. 'Yeah, you can. We can do anything and everything, as long as we are in it together, Ella. Are you saying yes, darling?'

'Absolutely.'

Ella kissed him, long and slow. Heat started to build between them and it was enhanced by love, by trust, by the knowledge that he was home, in the place he belonged, with the woman he loved.

His world, finally, made sense.

Ella slipped off his lap and held out her hand to him. He stood up, took it and they walked back to Hadleigh House, where Jabu had champagne waiting. She rested her temple against his upper arm and sighed. 'I can't believe that we've known each other less than three weeks. Technically, I just got engaged to my boss.'

Micah dropped a kiss on her head.

'Technically, I don't give a damn. You are here, we are together and that's all that matters,' he told her as he opened the door to his home.

Their home.

And the rest of their lives.

* * * * *

If you loved
The Powerful Boss She Craves
*then make sure to catch up on the first instalment
in the* Scandals of the Le Roux Wedding *trilogy*
The Billionaire's One-Night Baby
And look out for the final instalment, coming soon!

*In the meantime, don't miss out on
Joss Wood's other stories!*
How to Undo the Proud Billionaire
How to Win the Wild Billionaire
How to Tempt the Off-Limits Billionaire
The Rules of Their Red-Hot Reunion

Available now!

WE HOPE YOU ENJOYED
THIS BOOK FROM

H HARLEQUIN

PRESENTS

Escape to exotic locations where passion knows no bounds.

Welcome to the glamorous lives of royals and billionaires, where passion knows no bounds. Be swept into a world of luxury, wealth and exotic locations.

8 NEW BOOKS AVAILABLE EVERY MONTH!

#4041 THE KING'S CHRISTMAS HEIR
The Stefanos Legacy
by Lynne Graham

When Lara rescued Gaetano from a blizzard, she never imagined she'd say "I do" to the man with no memory. Or, when the revelation that he's actually a future king rips their passionate marriage apart, that she'd be expecting a precious secret!

#4042 CINDERELLA'S SECRET BABY
Four Weddings and a Baby
by Dani Collins

Innocent Amelia's encounter with Hunter was unforgettable... and had life-changing consequences! After learning Hunter was engaged, she vowed to raise their daughter alone. But now, Amelia's secret is suddenly, scandalously exposed!

#4043 CLAIMED BY HER GREEK BOSS
by Kim Lawrence

Playboy CEO Ezio will do anything to save the deal of a lifetime. Even persuade his prim personal assistant, Matilda, to take a six-month assignment in Greece...as his convenient bride!

#4044 PREGNANT INNOCENT BEHIND THE VEIL
Scandalous Royal Weddings
by Michelle Smart

Her whole life, Princess Alessia has put the royal family first, until the night she let her desire for Gabriel reign supreme. Now she's pregnant! And to avoid a scandal, that duty demands a hasty royal wedding...

HPCNMRA0822

#4045 THEIR DESERT NIGHT OF SCANDAL
Brothers of the Desert
by Maya Blake

Twenty-four hours in the desert with Sheikh Tahir is more than Lauren bargained for when she came to ask for his help. Yet their inescapable intimacy empowers Lauren to lay bare the scandalous truth of their shared past—and her still-burning desire for Tahir...

#4046 AWAKENED BY THE WILD BILLIONAIRE
by Bella Mason

Colliding with a masked stranger at a ball sends shy Emma's pulse skyrocketing. And that's *before* he introduces himself as Alexander Hastings, the CEO with a wild side, which puts him way out of her league! Will Emma step out of the shadows and into the billionaire's penthouse?

#4047 THE MARRIAGE THAT MADE HER QUEEN
Behind the Palace Doors...
by Kali Anthony

To claim her crown, queen-to-be Lise must wed. The man she must turn to is Rafe, the self-made billionaire who once made her believe in love. He'll have to make her believe in it again for passion to be part of their future...

#4048 STRANDED WITH HIS RUNAWAY BRIDE
by Julieanne Howells

Surrendering her power to a man is unacceptable to Princess Violetta. Even *if* that man sets her alight with a single glance! But when Prince Leo tracks his runaway bride down and they are stranded together, he's not the enemy she first thought...

HPCNMRB0822

SPECIAL EXCERPT FROM

Ⓗ HARLEQUIN
PRESENTS

*Colliding with a masked stranger at a ball sends
shy Emma's pulse skyrocketing. And that's before he
introduces himself as Alexander Hastings,
the CEO with a wild side, which puts him
way out of her league! Will Emma step out of the
shadows and into the billionaire's penthouse?*

*Read on for a sneak preview of Bella Mason's
debut story for Harlequin Presents,*
Awakened by the Wild Billionaire.

"Emma," Alex said, pinning her against the wall in a
spectacularly graffitied alley, the walls an ever-changing
work of art, when he could bear it no more. "I have to tell
you. I really don't care about seeing the city. I just want
to get you back in my bed."

He could barely believe that he wanted to take her back
home. Sending her on her way was the smarter plan. But
how smart was it really to deny himself? Emma knew the
score. This wasn't about feelings or a relationship. It was
just sex.

"Give me the weekend. I promise you won't regret it."
His voice was low and rough. He could see in her eyes

that she knew just how aroused he was, and with his body against hers, she could feel it.

"I want that too," she breathed.

"What I said before still stands. This doesn't change things."

"I know that." She grinned. "I don't want it to."

Don't miss
Awakened by the Wild Billionaire
available October 2022 wherever
Harlequin Presents books and ebooks are sold.

Harlequin.com

Get 4 FREE REWARDS!

We'll send you 2 FREE Books plus 2 FREE Mystery Gifts.

FREE
Value Over
$20

Both the **Harlequin® Desire** and **Harlequin Presents®** series feature compelling novels filled with passion, sensuality and intriguing scandals.

YES! Please send me 2 FREE novels from the Harlequin Desire or Harlequin Presents series and my 2 FREE gifts (gifts are worth about $10 retail). After receiving them, if I don't wish to receive any more books, I can return the shipping statement marked "cancel." If I don't cancel, I will receive 6 brand-new Harlequin Presents Larger-Print books every month and be billed just $6.05 each in the U.S. or $6.24 each in Canada, a savings of at least 10% off the cover price or 6 Harlequin Desire books every month and be billed just $4.80 each in the U.S. or $5.49 each in Canada, a savings of at least 13% off the cover price. It's quite a bargain! Shipping and handling is just 50¢ per book in the U.S. and $1.25 per book in Canada.* I understand that accepting the 2 free books and gifts places me under no obligation to buy anything. I can always return a shipment and cancel at any time by calling the number below. The free books and gifts are mine to keep no matter what I decide.

Choose one: ☐ **Harlequin Desire**
(225/326 HDN GRTW)

☐ **Harlequin Presents Larger-Print**
(176/376 HDN GQ9Z)

Name (please print)

Address   Apt. #

City   State/Province   Zip/Postal Code

Email: Please check this box ☐ if you would like to receive newsletters and promotional emails from Harlequin Enterprises ULC and its affiliates. You can unsubscribe anytime.

Mail to the **Harlequin Reader Service:**
IN U.S.A.: P.O. Box 1341, Buffalo, NY 14240-8531
IN CANADA: P.O. Box 603, Fort Erie, Ontario L2A 5X3

Want to try 2 free books from another series! Call 1-800-873-8635 or visit www.ReaderService.com.